One for sorrow, two for joy,
Three for a girl, four for a boy,
Five for silver, six for gold,
Seven for a secret never to be told,
Eight for a wish, nine for a kiss . . .

Also by Jenny Oldfield

One for Sorrow
Two for Joy
Three for a Girl
Four for a Boy
Five for Silver
Six for Gold
Seven for a Secret

Animal Alert 1–10
Animal Alert Summer: Heatwave
Animal Alert Christmas: Lost and Found

Home Farm Twins 1–20
Home Farm Twins at Stonelea 1–3
Scruffy The Scamp
Stanley The Troublemaker
Smoky The Mystery
Stalky The Mascot
Samantha The Snob
Home Farm Friends

Horses of Half-Moon Ranch 1–12

for a 8 Wish

Jenny Oldfield

Hodder
Children's
Books

a division of Hodder Headline

1

'You know your trouble, Sean Brennan? Emotionally speaking, you never grew up!'

Wham! The front door slammed shut and I scratched choice number seven from my mental list.

'Ouch!' Zoey cringed and hid her head under a pillow.

Connie opened my door an inch and peered downstairs, just at the precise moment Tammy Weinberg stormed back into the house.

'And another thing!' we heard her yell at my poor dad. (What did he ever do to her, for goodness sake?) 'The next time you date a girl, I recommend you keep your ex-wife out of the picture, OK!'

(So that's what he did. He talked about my mom. Big mistake, Dad.)

Tammy had given up on the relationship big time. She let my dad have it, down the full length of the hallway. 'Like I needed to know that Melissa's star sign was Sagittarius, her dress size was 8, and that despite the divorce you two still have a good thing going!'

'Ouch!' It was my turn to grimace.

Connie sighed and spied some more.

'I'm sorry . . .' Dad stammered. 'I thought you knew Melissa and I were still in contact over Kate.'

(That was me they were dragging into the contest. Ouch, ouch!)

Tammy was winning on points with all three judges. She was about to deliver the knockout punch. 'In contact, meaning Melissa coming across hot on the phone with, "Hi, darling!" and "Happy New Year, Sean baby!" '

Dad defended himself weakly. 'Melissa was at a party. She'd been drinking when she said that.'

Tammy thundered in with body blows. 'In contact, as in you cooing, "Hi, honey" back down the line, like she'd never screwed you for the house and alimony and all the rest!'

Tammy was a sports journalist; she knew how to sock a heavy punch.

And now the one that laid him flat. Ironically.

'How come you never learned to stand on your own two feet, Sean?' A right, a left, a scornful uppercut to the jaw. 'Like, you even allow your sixteen-year-old daughter to fix up your love life for you!'

A shocked silence from Dad. A gasp from me, still hiding behind my bedroom door.

'Yeah, I knew all along that Kate was the one who picked me out from the Lonely Hearts column, so there's no need to deny it . . . Like, you would ever have the nerve to do it yourself, Sean. Like, yeah!'

Wham! Slam! Exit one angry lady, with my dad laid flat on the canvas and out for the count.

'Let's face it: Tammy is ninety per cent accurate in her view of men,' Connie told us in all seriousness.

The house was quiet after the fight. Dad had picked himself up from the deck and retired to his own corner of the house. Connie, Zoey and me continued our New Year's Day sleepover with an in-depth 'guy' debate. It was past midnight, we were burning candles and drinking coffee to keep us awake.

'You mean, most guys are emotionally immature?' Zoey checked. 'Like, they don't know how to relate to girls at any significant level?'

I listened without comment, but I was thinking plenty. I had Joey Carter fixed in my mind all the time this discussion continued.

'When did you last have a guy genuinely tell you how he felt?' Connie challenged. Minus her mascara,

3

with her bleached blonde hair brushed smooth and flat, she looked all of twelve years old. Except for the body-piercing. 'In my experience, they always hide behind this big macho image – "Look at my muscles, watch me skate up this ramp and flip head over heels!" They just don't have the words to communicate "I love you," to take one important example.'

'Ziggy does,' Zoey countered, then blushed like she'd given too much away.

Ziggy and Zoey have been an item for six months. Ziggy is a high school basketball hero *and* emotionally liberated. Wow!

He's also Carter's best buddy, so I secretly hope he gives him lessons. It's been an age since I first felt stuff for Joey and he felt stuff for me. Result so far: zilch.

'Yeah, Zig's the exception,' Connie murmured.

'And my dad.' I made my first input. I had my blanket draped around my shoulders, my knees hunched up to my chest and my hands wrapped around a hot cup of coffee. The New Year had kicked in with sub-zero temperatures, and though the heating was on full-blast, the rooms in our old house were big and the system couldn't quite hack it.

'Your dad's cute, but he doesn't come across with the emotions,' Connie countered. 'Like, they're all zippered up behind his Mr Nice-Guy image.'

'That's not an image. That's how he is. He'd give you his last dime, I mean it.'

'Yeah, I like Kate's dad,' Zoey sighed sleepily.

Connie flashed her a look. 'I like him too. Don't get me wrong. But what's a good-looking guy like him doing five years into a divorce situation without a single meaningful relationship to his name? I mean, if it's not that he's closed himself off emotionally? You see what I'm saying?'

'I see, but I don't agree.' This was how it was between me and Connie. She has this outspoken manner which gets under my skin. I argue back. Zoey does her best to keep the peace. 'The problem is, he hasn't met the right woman yet.'

'Yeah, and why not?' Connie hung on to her point of view. 'Because he's all uptight. He works too hard. He keeps his feelings under wraps.'

'Whatever.' I shrugged and gave up.

'Sean deserves some love in his life,' Zoey said, all cuddled up inside her soft blue blanket.

'Which is why I made up this list in the first place!' I reminded them, waving the piece of paper with the scratched out names in their faces. Roberta, Marisa, Amy, Celia, Kristin, Meredith and now Tammy. Seven women all crossed off as total failures in my campaign to kick-start my lonely dad's love life.

Get this. I'd scanned the classified ads column in the *Fortune City Times*. Soul Mates: 'Attractive gal, fun-loving, young at heart seeks sensitive, intelligent guy for meaningful friendship.' I'd ringed around twenty box numbers, then narrowed it down to seven. Then I'd spent all last fall, right through to Thanksgiving, persuading Dad to take an interest in any one of the seven.

Finally, come December, when we'd eliminated all but one name – the rest were either too old, too young, too boring, too weird – he'd agreed to call Tammy and fix up a date.

That was two weeks back. He met her in a Mexican restaurant in Marytown, took her to a music club after the meal. Next day he told me it had gone fine. Tammy was witty, independent and fun to be with.

I was punching the air, crowing to everyone about my success. There were more restaurants. Tammy made a visit to the Angelworks studio, where my dad produces shows for Angel Christian, the big chat show host. She came to our place for Christmas dinner.

Which was the first time I actually met her. Think small and athletic, a dark-haired woman in her thirties who works out most days. She doesn't have any of the fluttery feminine stuff about her, and her dress code is sporty. Contemporary. And independent, like Dad said.

My only problem with Tammy was, she didn't come across with the emotions, as Connie would've put it. She was bright and breezy, full of confidence and jokes, but I couldn't work out what made her tick. Funny, huh?

What's more, I got the distinct impression she didn't like me much. Over the turkey and cranberry sauce, her eyes took in the dinner service, the quality of the wine, the name and rank of Dad's interior decorator. And that's how she treated me too: as part of the decor. Fine to look at but no interest in what lay behind my appearance. Like, no questions about my life, my pastimes, my school, my ambitions. A disappointment as a prospective permanent feature on my personal horizon, to tell you the truth.

So the fact that tonight she'd slammed the door on my dad and walked out on the soft furnishings and the wide screen TV didn't bother me much. Except for the fact that I'd run out of names on my list, and Dad was still Mr Lonesome.

Grando problemo. Five years was a long gap without love, and Dad was forty-two years old. Time waits for no man, even for a good-looking, grey-eyed, modest, shy, generous, warm-hearted guy like Dad.

Consider me prejudiced by all means. But believe what I tell you about him.

'So I really wish things would work out for him,' I told Connie and Zoey on our New Year sleepover.

New year, fresh start, big changes.

We'd gone to sleep at 3 am, woken halfway through January 2nd. Zoey had straightaway called Ziggy and gone off to meet him and Carter in the East Village McDonalds. Connie was presently at my bedroom mirror, reconstructing her hair with lashings of gel.

'Where's the point in just wishing?' she challenged. *Slick* with the gel, *flick* with the comb, assess the effect in the mirror. 'When did wishing for something to happen ever get anyone anywhere?'

Then I made my big mistake; I asked Connie for advice. 'So what do you suggest?'

'You make it happen,' she continued – *kink, pat, flick, smooth* – Connie's technique was that of a professional stylist. 'You set up a situation for your dad which he can't walk away from. In other words, you find him Ms Right.'

'So what d'you think I've been trying to do for the last three months?'

Connie glanced in the mirror at me standing directly behind her. 'Yeah, but your technique has been suspect.'

'Like, how?'

'Like you're using the wrong technology,' she explained carefully. 'Classified ads in a local newspaper; that's twentieth-century stuff. What you need to do is use the technology of the new millennium.'

'Like, what?' Connie was getting under my skin yet again. I watched her transform herself into rock-chick chic and saw myself looking boring behind her – dark hair hanging down around my shoulders, no mascara, no nose or eyebrow stud.

She answered me with over-the-top patience, as if teaching the word 'cat' to a two-year-old. 'Like, for instance, ditching the *Fortune City Times* and surfing the net for choice number eight.'

'The net?' I was kinda slow.

'Sure. You set up the search engine to log on to all the dating agency sites. You feed in the usual data – your dad's age, job, location – and see what compatible names come up.'

'They do that on the internet?'

9

'Sure they do.' Final *flick, tweak* and *pat*. The Hair was in position.

'How d'you know? Did you check out these sites?'

Connie dropped her gaze to fiddle in her purse for lip-gloss. 'Yeah, for fun,' she admitted. 'There's a whole huge industry built up on lonely hearts websites. And honestly, Kate, the kind of woman your dad needs is somebody modern and zappy enough to put herself about on the internet. Those sites attract the enterprising young professional types. Don't you see, it's perfect!'

'Hmm.' Slowly I was coming round to Connie's point of view. I grabbed a hair-clasp from my table and twisted my hair up on top of my head, chose a new black top (Christmas present from my mom), and my favourite pair of bootcut jeans. 'I guess.'

'Great!' Connie's personality gave no room for hesitation. 'Kate's New Year's Resolution: to find Sean's ideal woman on the net!'

'Maybe.' I curled my lashes up with mascara, pulled stray wisps of hair out of the clasp to make me look designer-dishevelled.

Meanwhile Connie pressed the power switch on my computer and logged on. 'Maybe-*schmaybe*!' she mocked. 'Just let's do it, OK!'

'Oh my God!' I gasped. I was stunned; my heart practically jumped out of my ribcage at what had just come up onscreen.

We'd clicked the wrong box. The Kismet web page had scrolled down on to Guys Seeking Gals section and we were reading stuff about eligible wranglers in Montana and lonely GIs posted abroad. And there, staring moodily at us from a passport-type photograph, was the face of Joey Carter. Thick, light brown hair, dark blue eyes, head to one side like he was asking the camera a question.

'I don't believe it!' Connie yelped.

I made my eyes focus on the information beside the picture. 'Joey Carter, called Carter by his friends. High school student majoring in having a good time. Six feet tall, 145 pounds. Into rock music and chicks who rate basketball as the ultimate physical and intellectual challenge.'

'How could he?' I choked over the words. I stood up from the desk and strode around the room. 'What a cheapskate! What a sad guy!' Really I felt betrayed, angry, hurt, confused. Did Joey really need to go to these lengths to find a girlfriend? Didn't he know, after all these months, how I felt about him?

Connie stayed by the screen, puzzling over the description. 'I never knew Carter was so into basketball,' she pointed out. 'Isn't that more Zig's thing?'

I suddenly stopped wearing out the carpet. 'Yeah!' I acknowledged. 'Carter goes to the big ball games, but he's not a fanatic.'

'So maybe Joey didn't feed the information into the Kismet site.' Connie was superbly logical when she needed to be. Her brain can cut through confusion like a knife through butter. I admire her for that. 'Kate, this could be some kind of wind-up!'

'Ziggy!' I ran back to the screen, re-read the info, recognised Carter's picture as the one he used on his student identity card. Zig could easily have stolen it for a couple of hours and e-mailed it to the website. 'This is his idea of a joke!'

'And Carter knows nothing about it!' Connie had begun to smile. The smile spread to a grin, then she started to laugh. She pressed more keys to print out a hard copy of what we saw onscreen. 'At least, not yet!' she giggled, seizing the print out and waving it in the air.

'What're you gonna do with it?' I watched Con stuff the sheet of paper into her purse and head straight for the door, torn between carrying on with the search for a girlfriend for my dad and going with Connie wherever it was she was headed.

'Let's just say I plan to eat brunch in McDonalds!' she told me.

With Zoey, Zig and Carter, no doubt.

'You coming?' she asked.

'No, I'll call a rain-check.' I chickened out. Just in case. I mean, maybe Joey did enter his details on to the website in all seriousness. If so, I didn't want to be around when he owned up.

So Connie split and I stayed home. I calmed myself with the routine task of clicking keys on the keyboard.

I soon found myself the Gals Seeking Guys section and scrolled through endless Corys, Shannas, Kims and Tiffanys.

'Hi. My name is Tiffany Pirkle. I'm twenty-eight years old, five-three tall and I weigh one hundred and eight pounds. I love to work out and line-dance. I'm looking for an older guy with no complications, living in his own place, who's fun to be with and who would welcome my pet Afghan, Sherpa, into his life. No meddlesome ex-wives or giant egos, please.'

Tiffany should be so lucky.

'Bridgitte Kohler . . . Beth Moran . . . Kari Bowers.' Kari was stunning, with green eyes, dark, glossy hair, and truly photogenic. I paused to remind myself that Dad didn't put good looks too high on his list of priorities. So I moved on.

'Heather Shaw, works in the fashion industry, owns a condo in Orlando, travels regularly to Europe . . . Elizabeth Grant, British but living stateside. Antiques buyer with a special interest in Italian paintings. Looking for a mature, sophisticated guy for interesting conversations over good French wine and food.'

Elizabeth Grant looked promising. Her picture showed a cool, beautiful face with clear, grey, almond-shaped eyes and a soft, full mouth. There was something about her style which I couldn't put my finger on – maybe the very good haircut, the fact that she didn't feel the need to grin toothily at the camera. Anyhow, interesting.

I looked twice, three times. Then I printed off the page and took it downstairs to show my dad. As Connie would say, you've gotta get right on in there and fight your corner. There's no use just gently wishing that things will work out.

2

This kind of stuff can stretch a friendship to breaking point, let me tell you.

Connie storms into McDonalds wearing face furniture and a wide grin. She waves a sheet of paper in front of me and demands, have I seen this?

It's a picture of me, with some 'Lurve for Sale' spiel beside it. I mean, where did that come from? I have no idea.

But Connie points the finger at Zig, who's halfway through his Big Mac. 'I suppose you think this is funny!' she says.

Zig chokes on his burger. He's obviously guilty.

Zoey realises what he did and lets him have it. 'Jeez, that is *so* immature!' she tells him. 'Going behind Joey's back and pulling that kind of stunt is juvenile. Don't you realise, people can get hurt?'

At which point Connie cuts in and tells us that Kate took it badly. She explains that they'd been surfing the net on behalf of Sean Brennan, and come across my ugly face in the Guys Seeking Gals section. Kate had jumped up and gone quietly crazy. Which is satisfying for me to know, but at the same time, not good, if you get what I mean.

Anyhow, it was definitely down to Ziggy.

The girls tossed their heads and refused to let us buy them a large Coke. They kept using words like 'insensitive' and 'Neanderthal' about guys in general. They utilised arguments they'd learned in Human Science to back up the theory that girls develop faster than boys and remain a superior species forever after. Then they adjourned to the rest room and left me and Zig sitting at the counter in awkward silence.

'Sorry,' Ziggy mumbled through a mouthful of bread and relish. 'It was a joke, OK?'

'Hah hah. How funny is it if I get back home to a whole heap of e-mails from women desperate for my body?'

'Pretty funny, actually.' Zig smirked.

I smirked back. 'Well, yeah . . .' The silence grew more comfortable. 'Weird how girls overreact to stuff,' I commented.

Zig munched away on Zoey's leftover burger. 'They call *us* immature,' he complained pleasantly. (Like, literally nothing upsets Zig except losing a big game.) 'But it seems to me they're mostly the ones who lose the plot.'

'I hate it when they fall to pieces and cry,' I confessed. But I was feeling kinda hypocritical. When, for instance, tears well up in Kate's eyes. I have great difficulty in stopping myself from putting my arms round her.

Plus, there's the fact that I definitely know I'm immature over my emotions connected with Kate. Not the emotions exactly, so much as my way of expressing them. Like, I feel the stuff deep down, but my tongue twists up inside my mouth and my arms and legs go like lead. Let's face it, I'm an illiterate in terms of feelings — worse than a baby, pretty much foetal as a matter of fact.

I sighed and pushed my recently bought plastic cup of Coke away from me.

Zoey and Connie returned and said they forgave us, so long as we guys learned our lesson not to mess around with Lurve on the Internet no more.

'Hey, I'm innocent,' I protested. 'Don't look at me.' Then I thought of a more definite way of arguing back. 'So, how come you and Kate are still interfering like crazy in poor old Sean's personal life?' I demanded. 'I mean, wouldn't you say that was pretty downright emotionally immature?'

'No way.' This pressed exactly the wrong buttons on Connie's mental keyboard. 'Kate and I talked the whole thing through. Sean's problem is that he's locked the door on his emotions, and what he needs is for someone to turn the key. This is our way of helping him do that!'

Connie's eyes shone with religious fervour. She really believed in what they were doing.

'Did you ask him what he thought?' Zig inquired. No hostility in the question, but Connie reacted like he'd stuck a knife between her ribs.

'So you think Kate should sit back and do nothing?' she demanded. Those evangelical eyes flashed with fury now. 'Don't you realise she cares deeply about her father? She sees him wasting his life. I mean, he's a good-looking guy for his age; he should have someone. Everyone deserves a share of happiness!'

You ought to know, Connie's a handful. The kind of girl who makes most guys run a mile. Yours truly in particular.

'Bull!' Zig came out with a surprisingly strong reply.

'I agree.' There's strength in numbers, so I grew brave enough to have my say. 'I may not know much about the way things work between the sexes,' I freely admitted, 'but I am sure about one thing: no way should Kate surf the net for a soul mate for Sean!'

'Oh right, Mr Relationship Expert!' Connie retorted, turning on me and speaking in a loud voice so that every Big-Mac-with-fries customer could hear. 'So you've given her the benefit of your immense wisdom, have you?'

My reply took me in way too deep. I knew this the moment I opened my big mouth. 'Not yet,' I said. 'But I sure will the next time I see her.'

So it was January, and we were partying at Zoey's house. Kate had been cool all during the evening. Cool Kate, as in 'frosty' and not speaking to me. But also cool, as in the way she looked. Which was dressed in a black party number, with straps and bare arms and stuff. Whatever she wore or exposed, she did it with style.

'Joey, you're a cute guy; how come you don't date on a regular basis?' Zoey's mom, Mrs Masterson, was the hostess for the evening. She'd drunk plenty of Jack Daniels and was growing close and confidential.

I backed off into a corner – bad move.

'I mean, I always felt it would be neat if you and Zoey got it together.' She went on breathing whisky fumes. 'That was before she and Ziggy became an item, naturally. Zig's a nice kid, but he's a little tall for Zoey, don't you think?'

I blinked and shrugged. What did you say?

'*Que sera sera*,' Mrs Masterson murmured, then sighed. She grew even closer and more confidential.

Help! I signalled to Sean Brennan who was passing nearby. I hoped he understood telepathy.

Luckily he did. 'Hey, Joey!' He came across and neatly stepped in between me and Alexis Masterson, offering me a glass of OJ and greeting me like he hadn't seen me for months. 'How come I haven't seen you round my place lately. Did you and Kate have a fight?'

'Aha!' Alexis pounced. She swung out of the corner and advanced unsteadily across the crowded room. 'I never knew Joey and Kate were an item! Hey, everybody, ain't that cute? Kate and Joey! Well, why didn't anybody tell me?'

'Because it's not true!' I heard Kate say above the music and the chat. Her stare turned from cool to sub-zero.

'Thanks,' I muttered to Sean.

'Seriously?' He looked worried about possible collateral damage.

'Yeah – for getting me out of a tight corner. Nope – for stepping up the arctic freeze between me and Kate.'

'Hmm.' Sean had been at the Jack Daniels bottle, but not as much as Alexis. He nodded at some other party guests: Connie and her parents, Ziggy's older brother, the cop, and my big sister, rock star Marcie. 'Why is she mad at you?'

I shrugged. 'Dunno.'

'Was it something about you appearing on a dating

agency website?' Sean acted like he recalled something of this nature.

'How did you know? Did she tell you?'

'Yeah. Kate's into all that stuff. As a matter of fact, she fixed me up with some woman called Elizabeth.' He still sounded vague and a little bit surprised that he'd agreed to it.

'No, really?' I figured this was illogical. Either Kate despised the website dating stuff, which made her what she thought of as justifiably angry with me for messing with it, or she didn't. You might not be on my wavelength here, but was I building up my case for when I confronted her – like later in the evening when she'd mellowed out.

'Yeah.' Sean glanced at his watch. 'Hey, that's where I should be right now!'

'Meeting this Elizabeth person?' I followed him across the room, watched him dig for his coat under a pile of others, trailed after him again to the door of the apartment.

'At Chez Georges, the French restaurant across town.' By this time Sean had begun to panic. 'Jeez, I'm gonna be late on our first date. Kate will give me such a hard time if I screw up after all the trouble she went to!'

And he was gone. Kate was standing separate from

the crowd, watching us, until Mel Wade stepped up and asked her to dance.

It was much later in the evening. The Mastersons' apartment was emptying out, leaving a trail of empty glasses, the remains of finger-food squashed into the carpet and a heap of unclaimed coats.

'For the last time, I didn't do it!' I yelled at Kate over the noise of the dishwasher working overtime in the kitchen. It was just me and her, the others were clearing up in the main room. 'It was Zig who put that data on the website!'

'So you keep telling me,' said Ms Iceberg. She stacked glasses on the drainer, ready to go in the dishwasher when it completed its cycle. 'But, one way or the other, I really don't care.'

I came between her and her obsessively neat stacking. 'That's not the way Connie and Zoey described it!'

'So Connie and Zoey are mindreaders now?' She brushed me aside and froze me with a look.

'Didn't they tell you it was Zig's idea of a joke?'

'And didn't you hear me say I really don't care?' *Stack-clink-stack-swoosh*, the dregs down the sink.

'OK, so how come you're so mad at me for supposedly subscribing to this Kismet thing, which by the way I didn't

22

do, when you're using the exact same method for finding some dumb date for your dad?' I pinned her down with my excellent logic, beat her at her own game.

She stared right through me. 'I'm not mad at you, Carter.'

'OK then, so you think it's OK to use this dumb method on Sean? Like, doesn't it occur to you that there are some weirdos out there paying into that website garbage so they can set up unsuspecting surfers?'

When Kate stopped stacking glasses, I knew I'd got through to her. 'Set them up how?'

'Hundreds of ways. For example, they date people so they can get their phone numbers and addresses, then quietly case their joints, move in and empty their houses of everything that isn't screwed to the floor . . .'

'No!'

'Yeah!' This was turning into a full-scale lovers' fight without the love bit. 'Get real, Kate. You could be doing Sean a whole heap of damage here!'

I never intended this remark to be in any way prophetic. I mean, I said it only to rattle the bars of Kate's cage, not because I thought it was true.

In nine hundred and ninety-nine cases out of a thousand I would've been wrong.

23

Sean would've raced across town on the Loop train to meet up with this Elizabeth Grant. Either she would've stood him up for keeping her waiting on a first date, or she would've hung around in a none too positive frame of mind.

In which case, conversation would've dragged. He would've looked at her sour-lemon face and decided no way did he want to get involved. She would've made up her mind that there were more punctual, thrusting and dynamic dolphins in the deep than Sean Brennan. He would've paid for her taxi home and they would never have seen each other again. End of story.

But unfortunately, not this time. Sean made it to Chez Georges a full ten minutes ahead of Elizabeth, who knew all about being fashionably late. The moment she showed up, she knocked him out with her classy good looks and English accent. She said 'larf' for 'laugh' and 'glars' for 'glass', called him 'dahling' and generally made a strong impression.

She dressed in designer labels without going over the top. The fact that all the waiters loved her when she spoke French to them didn't help Sean keep up his resistance to her charms. By the end of the evening he was hopelessly in love.

I learned this from Kate next day, Sunday, when she

suddenly made up her mind I was flavour of the month again.

In fact, she called at my house in Twenty-second Street before I'd even crawled out of bed. I heard my kid brother Damien answer the door, grab her and drag her inside. Two seconds later, Fern torpedoed into my room, tore off my blankets and signed wildly that Kate had arrived.

Fern is my adopted kid sister. She's mute, but she gets by pretty well with the lip-reading and the signing now that we got her into a good school. Some time soon, we hope to send her for state-of-the-art micro-surgery which will hopefully restore some hearing. Meanwhile, she rips off my bed linen and flashes me her wide white smile.

'OK, OK,' I groaned. 'What day is it?'

Fern held up seven fingers to show me it was Sunday.

'What time?'

Ten fingers show me 10 am.

'Tell Kate I'll be down in fifteen minutes,' I mumbled to Fern.

But the kid picked up my jeans from the floor and stuffed them into my hands. She grabbed my wrists and dragged me out of bed. Before I knew it, I was dressed and heading barefoot down the stairs.

Looking cool, I can tell you. I mean, sleep still in my

eyes, hair sticking up at a crazy angle, tongue coated with thick fur – yuck!

Kate was waiting for me in the basement, where Marcie and her band, Synergie, hang out and jam. Right now it was unused because Synergie had jetted off at 4 am on a world tour. She didn't remark on my disgusting appearance.

'Sorry,' she said. She was flopped on a Japanese mattress, her back supported by a sunshine yellow floor-cushion.

I was stunned by the apology. 'What for?'

'For giving you a hard time last night about the internet dating stuff.'

'No problem.' I shrugged, then made a futile attempt to smooth down my hair. 'Did Sean make it to the restaurant in time?'

And that was when Kate told me about the impression Elizabeth Grant had made on her dad. He'd arrived at his blind date and been totally and unexpectedly smitten.

'He hasn't stopped talking about her since the minute he got up,' she confided. 'It's "Elizabeth this", "Elizabeth that" . . . I had to come out of the house just for a break.'

'Talk about unlocking a guy's feelings!' I recalled Connie's phrase about Sean being zippered up emotionally speaking.

'Yeah!' Kate sighed and rearranged herself against the yellow cushion. 'Like, big-time!'

I sat down opposite on the bare floor. 'So I don't get it. Why aren't you celebrating? Isn't this working out the way you and Connie planned it?'

'Yeah.' She sighed again. 'But I can't get your comment out of my head, Joey. The one about me causing my dad problems. I mean, here he is, obsessed with this woman already, and he's only met her the one time.'

'You wish he'd take it more slowly?' *Like you and me*, I thought. Snail's pace in the romance stakes; that was Kate and me.

'I guess.' Listlessly she pulled at a corner of the cushion. 'You know something? I even got to thinking as I walked across town that maybe I'm jealous of this new relationship. I mean, if Dad spends all his time from now on with this new woman, where do I fit in?'

I felt this was a pretty honest and hard thing for Kate to own up to and I told her so. 'That's natural anyways, so you don't need to feel bad.' Mr Relationship Expert – yeah.

'But why didn't I expect it?' Kate was getting deep. I was shuffling forward to close up the gap between us. 'And there's something else I've been wondering.' She looked me in the eyes with a deeply troubled expression.

Up on the ground floor, in the hallway, I could hear Damien and Fern disturbing the peace. I gave myself ten seconds before they burst down into the basement. 'So?' I murmured.

'You know how you explained that some people use dating on the net in a bad way? Maybe to set up a serious theft situation, or maybe for some more weird reason.'

I nodded. Damien and Fern were getting louder.

Kate leaned forward. She bit her bottom lip and reached out to touch my hand. 'D'you think Elizabeth could be planning something like that?'

'No way. Forget I said it. I was out of line there. Listen, from what you tell me about Sean and her, it's probably the genuine thing; true romance!' If you think this was over-the-top reassurance, you would be right.

'Love at first sight.' Kate nodded and leaned back against the wall.

Damien flung open the basement door and took the stairs commando-style, with Fern close behind.

'But I still have a big question,' Kate confessed, ignoring the two kids for as long as she could. 'Why ever would a woman as perfect as Elizabeth Grant need to subscribe to Kismet in the first place?'

3

Things moved fast.

It had only been forty-eight hours earlier that I'd been wishing for a happy ending for my lonely dad.

'Calling any woman out there with intelligence, good looks, GSOH – a woman who can pass the Kate test.'

Now here we were, Sunday evening, and Elizabeth Grant was coming to dinner.

To say I was nervous doesn't quite cover it. I'd changed my clothes and my hairstyle three times, then finally settled for 501 jeans plus the most expensive Gaultier top I had in my closet! I figured this looked like I was making an effort but not exactly competing with our well dressed, sophisticated dinner guest.

My dad had done the cooking (Italian), chosen the wine (Spanish red), and arranged subdued lighting and flowers in the dining-room. He'd come to me for advice on dress-code and was looking, in my opinion, drop-dead gorgeous in a dark blue shirt and blue chinos, with brown loafers.

And now we were waiting for Elizabeth.

'How come she's always late?' I asked Dad, who was hovering by the dining-room window overlooking Constitution Square.

'Always, as in twice,' he reminded me. He glanced through the blinds as a car pulled up at the kerb, relaxing when he saw a taxi-cab drop someone off at the house next door.

'Shall I stir the pasta sauce?'

'Yeah – no, I just did.' Dad checked his wristwatch, fiddled with the blind some more.

So I took another look around the room. Low lamps cast mellow shadows on the mainly pale cream walls. They picked up the gloss on the rosewood dining-table and reflected in the cut-glass wine goblets set out beside the three immaculate place settings. There was even a dull metal urn filled with red roses as a centrepiece and tall white candles in pewter holders waiting to be lit.

All this was stuff that would impress a British antiques dealer: eighteenth century furniture to match a rare example of original Fortune City architecture, dating way back to when the American Constitution was first signed.

These days, the city was mostly a forest of concrete

and glass tower blocks like any other place. We'd ridden on the back of the micro-chip boom of the seventies and eighties and become a centre for modern financial systems. We also have a good college, which means twenty-four-hour bookstores, late night movies and big summer rock concerts in the park. Not a bad place to be, all in all.

Not that this was at the forefront of my mind as I messed with the place settings and we went on waiting. I was thinking more about my morning's conversation with Carter.

He'd answered my big question about how come Elizabeth needed to date on the internet by reminding me that even someone as fantastic as my dad had been lonely and lovelorn until I made the move for him.

'Maybe Elizabeth has a daughter doing the same kind of thing for her,' he suggested. 'Y'know; a recent divorcee with her kid looking out for her.'

I'd taken this on board, but told Carter I didn't know the first thing about Elizabeth Grant's personal circumstances. 'All I know from her picture on the Kismet site is that she's gorgeous, and from my dad that she's the greatest thing to happen in this world since the invention of the wheel.'

Still, I wasn't prepared for the impact she made

when she finally did turn up at our door.

The bell rang and dad rushed to answer it, with me standing in the dining-room doorway.

She stood there in a wrap-around, ankle-length camel coat, a light, leopardskin print scarf around her neck. She wore a dark, brimmed fur hat, so expensive that it was impossible to tell if it was fake or genuine. Fake, I hoped. And she smiled at my dad in a special, warm way; a little bit surprised at herself to be here so soon after they'd met, but close and intimate nevertheless.

You can pick up a lot of meaning in a brief smile if you concentrate.

Dad held out his hand and guided her over the threshold. He took her coat, and when she swept her hat from her head, her dark blonde hair fell to chin-length in a silky soft curtain. Under the coat she wore a velvety claret top and black trousers. Her jewellery – necklace and matching earrings – was gold set with garnets or maybe even rubies to pick up the colour of her top.

I don't need to tell you that Elizabeth Grant was also fashion-model skinny. But what you won't predict is the way she stepped past Dad to greet me for the first time.

She came and took my hands, kissed me on both cheeks. Well, air-kissed; the European stuff. My lips brushed her cheek and I smelt perfume so exclusive I didn't recognise it.

'Kate!' Elizabeth smiled all over me. Not cheesy, but gracious and refined. 'Sean told me he had a daughter, but he didn't mention how gorgeous you were.' She turned to him. 'She's beautiful, darling. You must be so proud.'

So first impressions were favourable all round, I guess.

And she loved the house too.

'Exquisite!' she kept saying. Her tapered fingers would touch the gilt frame of a mirror in the hallway or a bronze head in an arched alcove in the dining-room. 'Marvellous, wonderful!'

Elizabeth took a cocktail glass from me with a warm, sisterly look which jumped me into assuming that I'd known her for longer than five minutes. She sipped at it without leaving a lip-gloss smear on the rim.

And Dad ran around like crazy – would she like this, would she like that? What type of music did she prefer to listen to?

'Opera,' she replied. 'Anything except *La Traviata*, which makes me too sad for words!'

We laughed as if we sympathised with this. To be up front, I didn't know my *Trav* from my *Cats*.

Then we sat down to dinner and talked. Or rather, Elizabeth was the one who made the running, talkwise. She gave us her whole history over the linguine.

'I'm setting up a US arm of a well-known British antiques and fine art dealership. It's a firm that has been in existence since the middle of the nineteenth century. You both must have heard of Nicholsons?'

Dad and I faked it by nodding. Sure, everyone knew Nicholsons. (Never even heard of it, actually.)

'My specialist area is still-life painting, though I'm also strongly drawn to features of earlier vernacular architecture, particularly over here in New England and the mid-West. So I aim to set up a US team which can scour the country for wood and stone carvings that might have been set into ancient lintels over farmstead doorways or across chimney breasts; that kind of thing.'

I felt my eyes glaze over. To me this sounded like one big yawn. But Dad was still bright-eyed and bushy-tailed.

'Of course, it's a big challenge to get into the American market. Rupert, my boss over in London, has given me just twelve months to get it off the ground. And it seems to me that the way the internet is used over here, that may well be the key to both finding and selling high quality antiques.'

'Surfing the net,' Dad agreed. *Nod, nod; yes, yes.*

Which reminded me of Kismet, and maybe explained how come Elizabeth had signed on. After all, she was new to the country, using the net to set up a business. In that situation it would seem like a logical move to surf for promising boyfriend material. And wow, had Elizabeth hit lucky first time! Dad was a media man working for the most famous chat show host in the world. A kind, gentle, considerate guy. Oh, and gorgeous too.

Who says fairy tales never happen in real life?

Over the spearmint and chocolate gelati I found myself warming to the whole idea of Elizabeth and my dad.

'School in England is so different,' she told me. 'In America, when you say "public school", you mean schools that are funded by the government. Over there, it means that your parents fork out huge amounts of money to send you away to be educated in private establishments. You wear a strict and horribly unfashionable school uniform, and you're extremely lucky if you bump into a member of the opposite sex more often than once a week.'

'No, really?' I gasped. This sounded primitive.

'Yes, really!' Elizabeth laughed. 'At least, that was the case until a few years ago, when even the public school system had to acknowledge that, wonder of wonders, boys and girls do in fact enjoy being in each other's company.'

I zoned out here. She was going on about a college in someplace called Barth and a weird game called lacrosse. Dad seemed interested though.

'Lacrosse?' he quizzed.

And Elizabeth ran smoothly into another long explanation. 'A game played with sticks which have shallow, triangular nets at one end . . .'

I give her this much: she sure could talk.

Until my mom put in an unannounced appearance, that is. Then there was this deep, sudden silence.

'Melissa!' Dad broke it by jumping up from the dinner table.

'Mom!' I squeaked, for some reason feeling hot with guilt.

I mean, my parents had been divorced for years. They led their own lives: Mom in New York where she set up an art gallery, Dad here in Fortune City in the same old production job with Angelworks.

'Sean?' Elizabeth said quietly, quizzically, as if she deserved an explanation.

Dad rescued the chair that he'd sent rocking backwards as he jumped up. 'Er – Elizabeth, I'd like you to meet my ex-wife, Melissa. Melissa, this is Elizabeth Grant. She's from England.'

'Oh, you're English!' Mom advanced across the room. She dropped her purse from her shoulder on to the floor, sighed and kicked off her heeled shoes, like she was utterly at home. 'That's nice!'

Elizabeth, who looked as if nothing ever disturbed her poise, stood up and gave Mom the air-kiss nonsense. 'I'm so pleased to meet you.'

'What happened?' Dad yelped, using the table as a barrier between himself and the two women.

'What d'you mean, what happened? I can call to see my own daughter, can't I?'

'But why aren't you ski-ing in New Hampshire with Scott Elliot?'

'I was. Not enough snow, so we came away early and reserved a suite in the Metropole so I could drop in and see Kate.' Mom studied Elizabeth's rubies and the classically beautiful sweep of her chin and cheekbones. Dad's new woman registered a close challenge to her own well preserved, wrinkle-free face. 'Where did you and Sean meet?' she asked sweetly, though it was obvious she was about to inflict the third degree.

'At Chez Georges.' Elizabeth's reply skilfully ducked the potentially embarrassing issue of Kismet. 'It's so nice to run into someone with similar tastes and interests when you're in a new city, don't you think?'

'And what brings you to Fortune City, Elizabeth?' Mom went on. She had steel in her voice and her smile was rapidly turning rigid.

'Fine art and antiques. Sean tells me you run a small gallery, Melissa, so it seems we may have a good deal in common.'

Not so much of the 'small', I thought. Mom also sensed the put-down and her smile grew positively mask-like.

'Fine art?' she echoed. Then, 'Antiques? Do you buy here and ship the stuff back to England, or the other way around?'

'Both. But let's not talk shop or we'll bore poor Sean and Kate.'

Mom ignored this. 'So who do you work for: Sothebys? Christies?'

'Nicholsons,' Elizabeth told her. 'I deal mainly in nineteenth-century oils. It's probably not your area, Melissa.'

'Nicholsons?' Mum repeated almost everything Elizabeth told her. She drew out the name in three long, separate syllables and let it drift around the room. Then she suddenly switched topics to tell me about her après-ski parties in New Hampshire, where she'd met everybody who was anybody.

I noticed Dad and Elizabeth take up their glasses and fade gratefully into the small sitting room leading off from the dining area.

As soon as they were gone, Mom whipped me out into the hallway and put me through the inquisition.

'How did your father *really* meet that woman?' she hissed. 'You can't seriously expect me to believe that he just ran into her at that absurdly overpriced French restaurant!'

With Mom there was no point even trying to evade the issue. 'I found her for him on the internet,' I confessed.

Which made her evening big time. 'That's so sad!' she crowed, with the widest of smiles. 'Poor Sean!'

I frowned and warned her to keep her voice down. 'You're only acting this way because you're jealous!' I whispered.

'Me? Jealous! Really, Kate!'

'Why else would you twist the knife into Elizabeth the way you did?'

'No, you've got it all wrong, honey. I have my life and your father has his. What he does with his relationships is his business. Only – the internet! That does look a little weird, you have to admit.'

'Elizabeth's OK,' I told her stubbornly.

Mom's eyes widened. 'You mean you like her?'

'Yeah, she's good fun.' If a little egocentric. But I didn't share this with Mom.

'Well, I give the whole thing exactly one week,' she declared, real loud this time.

'Shh! Dad's gonna be mad if they overhear this.'

'He likes her? Here I was supposing that he couldn't wait to ditch her as soon as it was decently possible.' Mom grew goggle-eyed. 'What happened to the good taste he had when he married me?'

'Mom, you're the pits!' I ran for her shoes and purse and crammed them into her arms. 'Go back to your boyfriend and your nice warm hotel suite. Come and see me tomorrow when you learn to behave properly!'

She let me bundle her towards the door, then turned. 'What's her second name again?' she quizzed.

'Grant,' I muttered through clenched teeth. 'Now go, Mom, go!'

* * *

I got a phone call from her next morning.

'Hi, honey, it's me. Did that woman stay over last night? What did she say about me? Is your father still infatuated by her?'

'Mom, it's not your business.' As a matter of fact, Elizabeth had risen magnificently above Mom's shock arrival and sudden departure. She'd kept her poise, talked on through the evening about England and her home town of Barth, where her college was also based.

She'd left at eleven-thirty after Dad had called a cab and arranged a third date with her for Wednesday night, this time at the bistro inside the Foster Museum of Modern Art.

'Hmm.' Mom's instinct and my silence told her everything she needed to know. 'Well, listen, Kate, Sean may change his mind once you pass on what I'm about to tell you.'

'Mom, what're you saying?' This was no joke. This was petty jealousy taken one step too far, even for Mom.

'I've spent an hour on the phone this morning,' she went on. 'I called New York and spoke to a few friends in the fine art world. I even called Nicholsons in London, but all I got was an answer machine, because of course it's the middle of the night over there.'

41

'What for? What d'you hope to find out?'

Mom took her own time to dish the dirt. 'No luck with London, but there is a branch of Nicholsons situated just off Park Avenue. I spoke to the guy there, told him that I suspected there was a British woman over here who was making false claims about having a professional connection with them.'

'Jeez, Mom!' I couldn't believe that spite could drive a person this far.

'Just listen. I gave the guy in the office Elizabeth's name. And surprise – he never heard it before!'

'But . . . !' This wasn't a fully formulated response, but it was all I could come up with at the time.

'You hear me, Kate? Tell your father that there's no Elizabeth Grant working for Nicholsons Fine Art Dealers. The woman he picked up on the internet is an out-and-out fake!'

4

Kate and I were back.

I mean, we were a team again. She was coming to me for help over the Elizabeth Grant situation, and I was resisting the 'told you so' temptation.

We were doing what we both know we do best. Sleuthing, spying, deducing, shadowing. Philip Marlowe, eat your heart out!

Monday, Kate called me and asked to meet at the gates of City Park.

'Jeez, Carter, I don't know what to do,' she told me. There was frost an inch thick on the park railings, the sky was a deep, clear blue. 'According to my mom, Elizabeth Grant doesn't exist!'

She explained the Nicholsons mystery as we walked towards Monument Hill.

'Let's face it, this could be your mom acting out of insane jealousy; end of story,' I pointed out. 'How sure can we be that she's not just spreading unpleasant rumours?'

'I already figured that,' Kate admitted. Her feet crunched along the icy walkway, up the wide steps towards the marble monument. 'So I checked out the New York branch of Nicholsons myself, and I got the same answer: no one there has heard of Elizabeth Grant.'

'But you say she's just taken the job?' Falling in alongside Kate, we took the steps two at a time. 'So if this Nicholsons dealership is a big multi-national organisation, it could be that the US base isn't on message yet as regards all recent employees.' I for one doubted Melissa Brennan's motives and wasn't willing to jump to conclusions.

'Possible,' Kate agreed. But she wasn't convinced. For a while she sat on the low wall by the monument, distracted by a bunch of colourful, noisy kids tobogganing down the steep hill.

'Next stop, Cyberama!' I announced. I can be assertive when Kate is wobbling, and vice versa. That's why we make a good team, detection-work-wise.

I led her out of the park, back on to Constitution Hill, where we jumped on the Circle Train for a couple of stops into the city centre, and off again, straight into the chrome-counter atmosphere and ground-coffee aroma of the town's major internet cafe.

*   *   *

Two cappuccinos later, we were sitting by a screen.

'How old is Elizabeth Grant?' I asked Kate.

'The Kismet database gives it as thirty-five.'

'Say thirty-eight to forty.' I made allowances for poetic licence on Elizabeth's part, then did some rapid calculations in my head. All the while I kept on pressing keys for search engines to direct me to the data I needed. 'Which school in England did she attend?'

Kate screwed up her eyes in concentration, then came up with a name. 'Barth Ladies College.'

B-A-R-T-H. I logged on to a site giving me Major British Schools, then clicked the keyboard. Zilch. No such number, no such name.

'Try it without the R,' Kate suggested. 'Try Bath, as in hot tub.'

B-A-T-H. Bath Grammar School. Bath Ladies College. Yes!

I used the mouse to scroll down all the preliminary stuff about where the place was, how old it was, how many students on roll. Then we came to fees.

'Wow!' Kate stared. 'They spend that kind of dough in England to get their kids through high school?'

To us, it looked worse than Yale or Princeton.

'Ignore that,' I told her. 'What we need is a list

of names relating to the school roll way back, when Elizabeth was there.'

I brought up staff names, ex-principals going back a hundred years. Miss Simpson, Miss Bartholomew (with an R), Miss Worthington and Miss Proudie.

'Maybe the site doesn't list ex-pupils,' Kate murmured. We both had our faces practically glued to the screen.

'Alumni . . .' I muttered, clicking the mouse against the strange word. 'Hey, this is it – lists of ex-students, year by year. They don't give anything except a name and contact number for the whole group; otherwise, no address or phone number. It's just a record of who attended.'

'Good enough.' Now that she understood what I was doing, Kate grew more excited. 'Scroll back twenty-five years and we should get to the period when Elizabeth was there.'

'*If* she was there.' I heavily stressed the first word. Then we sat in silence as we read one list of names after another.

We had to go a couple of years further back than we'd calculated until we reached the list we wanted.

'There!' Kate stabbed at the screen with her forefinger. 'Elizabeth Grant! So the school bit's true!'

She existed – below Jayne Graham, above Jacinta

Halford and Sara Hyde Smith. And yeah, working it out, she must be all of forty years old now.

'She looks good for forty,' Kate thought out loud. 'And British women don't even believe in cosmetic surgery. Mom would scratch her eyes out if she knew.'

By this time we'd left Cyberama and were skidding on the knobbly, trodden-down ice along the sidewalk where the salt wagons hadn't yet been.

'So she's lying about the antiques dealers, but she's telling the truth about her school.' In my jacket pocket I carried a folded sheet of paper – a print-out of the relevant list from the Bath Ladies College website.

'Do I tell Dad?' Kate asked.

'If you don't, you can bet Monopoly dough that Melissa eventually will,' I pointed out.

'Yeah, but not right away. Dad's refusing to talk with Mom after the way she behaved last night. So if Mom wants to personally dish the dirt on Elizabeth, she's gonna have to put it down in writing and send it through the post!'

'OK, so that gives us a couple of days. So don't tell him anything yet. Let's find out more information before we ruin his perfect romance.' I felt good with our progress to date and was looking forward to a little light detective work with Kate to break us into a new year. It was time for us to sleuth. Is there such a word? 'I sleuth, you sleuth, he sleuths'?

'OK, so this is the plan!' Kate came up with an idea that took my limited acting ability right to the wire.

I mean, Jeez, I'm a blue-collar kid from Marytown. My mom works at a supermarket checkout, my dad gets his hands dirty fixing auto engines. And what Kate was suggesting was that I showed up at Elizabeth Grant's place claiming to be a friend of Kate's who was interested in taking up a career in fine art when I left school. With my accent and general lack of class? Like, yeah.

'You can do it, Carter!' Kate insisted.

'Let me get this straight. I go to Elizabeth for careers advice?'

'Correct. I'll come along to hold your hand, so to speak.'

'When?' I faltered. The idea of going anywhere hand in hand with Kate was unnerving.

'Wednesday,' she said. 'I'll fix it for you to meet up with Elizabeth at her office in Century Tower, before she goes off to the art gallery for the date with Dad.'

'Why are we doing this?' I double-checked when Wednesday came. Maybe I was being slower than I normally am.

'So that we can poke around the place, pick up office stationery, read noticeboards, get a feel of who it is that Elizabeth really works for.'

'Gotcha.' I nodded. We were crossing the plaza facing on to Fortune City Hall, heading for Century Tower, which had won an architecture prize back in the 1990s. The whole facade was shaped like a shallow rectangular dish, all twenty storeys of it, and fashioned out of smoked glass and steel. It was expensive real estate, so only the great and the good rented office space here.

'She's expecting us,' Kate reminded me. 'I told her you were crazy about the French Impressionists and wanted her angle on how to get over to Europe to study.'

'I am? I do?' Monet/Manet/Renoir – it was all identical smudges of paint to me. Kate had tried to educate me in the past thirty-six hours, but my progress had been zilch.

'Yeah. Who was the guy who painted everything as groups of tiny dots?' she quizzed.

'Renoir.'

'No; Pissaro. Who painted sunflowers?'

'Degas.'

'No; Van Gogh. And he wasn't French, he was – something else, maybe Dutch. One of those tiny places that you can fit inside Texas. Degas painted ballet dancers.'

'OK, OK, enough!' We entered through the automatic

doors into the giant foyer of Century Tower. 'You're making me nervous, so let's just quit it and take it as it comes.'

Up in the elevator to the tenth floor, as Elizabeth had directed. Out into a wide, shiny lobby and left down a long corridor. Secretaries and PAs wafted by. We passed the polished nameplates of attorneys, ad men and literary agents, made our way to suite 108, where the sign on the double door said 'Elizabeth Grant, Fine Art Dealer'.

No mention of Nicholsons.

'This all feels OK,' I mumbled to Kate as we pressed the security button then pushed the door in Reception.

'OK' meaning serious art on the walls, thick carpets, a bank of telephones, computers and fax machines.

Elizabeth's secretary was a small, red-haired woman wearing a short haircut and the latest craze in eyeglasses. She recognised who we were and buzzed her boss, who said, sure, send them in.

So we found ourselves in her office, breathing in cream leather and chrome armchairs, facing Sean's new girlfriend across a wide glass desk.

'Hi!' she said in a welcoming way, even though she was busy speaking down the phone. She gestured for us to park our butts on the soft kidskin.

We overheard some wheeler-dealing – prices were haggled over, names dropped, exhibition space measured

– and meanwhile we took in more of the office atmosphere.

There were paintings of a French cathedral at dawn, and the same one at midday hung side by side behind Elizabeth's desk, one of a round vase of blue flowers across the room. It felt like there was big money in these objects, and so far everything was as it should be.

But why no Nicholsons sign on the door after what Elizabeth had told Kate and her parents?

'Rupert, listen, I have people here now.' Elizabeth brought the phone conversation to an end. 'Is it OK with you if we tie up the loose ends at a later date? . . . Yah, OK, fine.'

This was some voice, I can tell you. Real classy. Likewise the looks. Kate had told me how glossy magazine good-looking her dad's girlfriend was, but seeing has to be believing.

She wore a dark blue, sleeveless shift dress with a matching jacket hooked over the back of her chair. And she paid attention to details, like the colour of her nail polish matched her lipgloss and neither was garish. Her blonde hair might have been from a bottle, but if so it was the best bottle on the market. Kate had taught me to notice stuff like this.

'So you're Joey Carter,' she said to me, reaching across

the desk to shake my hand. She smiled as if she really meant it, but also as if she'd had a lot of practice at genuine, welcoming smiles. 'Kate was really eager for us two to meet.'

I mumbled something about wanting to major in fine art at college. 'Or maybe travel to Europe for a year to look at some galleries,' I added. 'Kate says you know all about that.'

'That's right, I do. And my advice would be to do a couple of years at college before you do the travel bit, so that at least you have some knowledge behind you.' Elizabeth was patient and did us the favour of taking me seriously, whatever impression she had of me from across the desk.

I cleared my throat, nodded, crossed my ankle over my knee and tried to clasp it in relaxed mode. Then the part came that I'd been dreading.

'What's your favourite period in painting?' she asked me, her grey eyes calm and steady on my twitching face.

'Um, I guess the French Impressionists. Degas and all that stuff.'

'His horses or his dancers?'

'Erm, dancers.' (Wrong answer. Did I look like a guy who spent his free time studying pictures of girls in tutus? I don't think so.)

52

Kate sat stiff beside me, waiting for me to make my first major mistake.

But we were saved by the secretary in the glasses, who came into the room to tell Elizabeth that she had a client named Brown waiting in Reception to see her.

Elizabeth thanked the secretary, Monica, then excused herself to Kate and me. 'Sorry about this. Mr Brown doesn't have an appointment, but what he does have is a few million spare dollars in the bank!' she said with a smile. She slipped out of the room after Monica, leaving a whiff of perfume and a faint hum of air-conditioning.

'What do you think?' Kate whispered, hardly waiting for the door to close.

'She seems like the real thing to me.'

'So maybe she did work for Nicholsons until very recently, but she split from them,' I said, taking in the view of the city tower-blocks through the convex-smoked glass. 'Or else her job is so new, that the name plate hasn't gone up on the door yet. Like we said before, these multi-nationals have poor internal communication.'

I was vaguely wondering how many millions of dollars the blue flowers in the bronze vase painting was worth when Kate stretched across Elizabeth's desk to read the phone numbers scribbled on a notepad. She read out the name at the top of the list: 'Rupert Ecclestone – 212 717 6669'.

Easy to remember, so I retained that one, no problem. 'So?' I asked.

'Elizabeth mentioned that her boss was called Rupert. This is a New York number. But her guy's supposedly based in the London branch of Nicholsons.'

I shrugged while Kate flicked through other stuff on the desk. She gasped when she lifted a pile of A4 copy paper and unearthed two small, dark red booklets bearing the gold shield and lion and unicorn motif of the British passport. 'Two!' she said, probably louder than she'd intended.

Two passports? Elizabeth's and her daughter's? Elizabeth's and Monica's? Elizabeth's and a husband we didn't know about? Worth following up, for sure.

So Kate picked one up and slid the other towards me. I flicked through the pink pages to the back and checked the photograph of Elizabeth. Then I read through the details – Grant, Elizabeth, British citizen, place of birth and so on.

'Hey!' Kate's voice was loud again. 'Look at this!'

I leaned across and saw a photograph of a woman who looked similar to Elizabeth, except with dark hair and glasses. The details read; Hyde Smith, Sara,

British citizen . . . 'That doesn't add up,' I muttered. 'Why would Elizabeth be carrying another woman's passport?'

'Hyde Smith?' Kate frowned. 'Where did I hear that name before?'

'Most people get by with one passport and one name.' I took the two of them and compared them. Total mystery.

'Carter, where's that list?' Kate demanded.

'What list?'

'The print-out from Bath Ladies College.' She dived her hand into my jacket pocket and drew it out. 'Sophie Goode, Jayne Graham, Elizabeth Grant, Jacinta Halford, Sara Hyde Smith . . . !'

I stared at the passports to make sure there was no error. I got it as straight as I could in my head: either Elizabeth Grant was assuming the identity of her ex-school buddy, Sara Hyde Smith, to make it through immigration, or vice versa. The big question was, why? And what had happened to the real Sara or the real Elizabeth?

Kate and I were so into the whole weird situation that we failed to notice the office door open or see Monica walk back in.

'Elizabeth asked me to give you a message,' the secretary said.

I stashed the two passports behind my back, looking guilty as hell.

'She says she's sorry to mess things up, but she has to go out with Maurice Brown to look at a painting. She wonders if she could talk to Joey about his plans some other time.' Monica's gaze cut through us like a knife. She knew I was hiding something from her.

I eased the passports into the back pocket of my jeans, trying to act casual, but feeling my face turn bright red. 'That's fine,' I mumbled. 'Thanks.'

Ms Monica's glasses flashed in the reflected light from the desk lamp as she hustled forward to lift her boss's blue jacket from the back of her chair. If Kate and I had guilt written over us, the secretary had sharp, mean suspicion. 'I'll show you out,' she offered. Meaning: 'I wouldn't trust you two as far as I could throw you!'

So we had to leave. And I had no chance under Monica's eagle eye to extract the passports from my pocket and slip them back on to the desk.

We didn't see any sign of Elizabeth or Mr Brown as we left, and Kate and I didn't talk until we were in the elevator. Then I hitched the passports out of my jeans.

It took Kate a couple of seconds to log on to the stupid truth. 'Jeez, Carter!' she said.

'I know.' I felt my shoulders sag. 'So this is another great mess I've gotten us into.'

5

'Major dilemma,' I told Connie on the phone. 'Do I tell Dad everything we've found out about Elizabeth Grant and ruin his romance? Or do we keep right out of it?'

'You say this woman is carrying a fake passport?' Connie checked.

'That's how it looks. And you know what? Carter only walked out of her office with both of the darned things in his back pocket! You won't believe what we went through to get them back on her desk.'

'So tell me.' Connie took a philosophical view. I could picture her settling back in her chair, like she was getting ready to chat about the latest episode in her favourite soap opera.

I needed to get this out into the open; I'd been so mad at Carter that we'd had another fight. 'We were in the elevator and he holds up the passports. I'm saying, "Oh, Jeez, we have to put them back before anyone knows they're missing!" Carter's mumbling about maybe going back up and hanging around until we see Monica the secretary leave work. 'Then how do we get in through a locked door?' I ask.

'So Carter has another bright idea. He knows a guy who works as a courier, delivering packages. He gets him on his cell-phone, asks him to ride over to Century Tower with a fake delivery. This is so we can draw Monica, the secretary from Hell, down to Reception to pick up a non-existent package. Meanwhile, Carter and I sneak the passports back inside Elizabeth's office.'

'Neat!' Connie approved this tactic. 'Did it work?'

'Nope. Carter's courier friend said it was more than his job was worth.' I recalled the disappointment we'd experienced until I said, why didn't Carter borrow a motorcycle helmet and go up to Reception himself, impersonating a courier.

When I filled Connie in on this move, she laughed. 'How did he look in the helmet? I bet he was cool.'

'Con, get serious. Finally, Joey finds himself a helmet via Ziggy's basketball coach, Tom Vernon. By this time, everyone's leaving the building to go home for the evening. So Carter dons the helmet and zooms across the foyer to Reception, asking for Monica, saying it's urgent.'

'And this time it worked?' Connie wanted me to fast

forward. 'You snuck in to the office while she was out?'

'Yeah. She left so fast, she overlooked the security locks on the door, so I could get in and out again, no problem.'

'And you're in the clear?'

'Technically, yeah. But that Monica's a majorly-suspicious employee. She knows someone played a trick on her about the courier stuff. And my feeling is she'll pass on her doubts about Carter and me to Elizabeth.'

'Deny everything!' Connie recommended dishonesty as the best tactic. 'Make out like Monica's acting paranoid. I find that usually works.'

'OK, so what do I do now?' I got back to my main dilemma. 'Do I tell Dad everything?'

'And burst his bubble?'

'Yeah, I know. He's really happy over this Elizabeth thing.'

'He won't thank you for butting in,' Connie warned. 'Believe me, Kate, you could build up a case for Elizabeth being a major war criminal, but if Sean's blinded by passion, he's never gonna believe you.'

'I know,' I sighed again. 'Listen, Con, thanks. I can't talk any more; I just heard Dad come home. Catch you later.'

I'd put down the phone when Dad came humming

upstairs. The tune was some corny love song that had topped the charts before Christmas. It was called 'Needing You', and it made my heart sink that this was the tune Dad had floating in his head after his date at the art museum with Elizabeth. The way things seemed to be headed, I thought some tragic aria from one of her favourite operas might be more suitable.

'Hey!' he said when he poked his head around my door.

'Hey. Did you have a good time?'

'The best!' he smiled. 'Elizabeth is just the wittiest, most charming woman. When she walks into a room, everyone turns to watch her. She's like a magnet. I mean, she's just so stunning. And intelligent and classy . . .'

'Great,' I said in a flat voice. 'I'm happy for you, Dad.'

'Yeah, and it's all down to you,' he grinned, overlooking my lack of enthusiasm, maybe putting it down to the fact that I was tired. 'Kate, honey, I owe you one big, big thank you for hooking me up with Elizabeth Grant!'

I took the train early next morning to the school sports arena. Even though we were on vacation, I knew that this was where I would find Carter.

Sure enough, he'd joined in the coaching session with Ziggy and the team. He was wearing a loose T-shirt and shorts and a pair of battered trainers, looking about half the size of some of the giant attackers.

'Hey, Carter!' I called from the sidelines.

A kid who was six-four in height and weighing almost two hundred pounds shimmied past three opponents, leaped and pushed the ball into the net. His buddies gave him a high-five as he loped back to centre court.

'Carter!' I hissed, while coach Vernon pulled players off and put new ones on. Joey was among the ones he wanted to rest.

He finally heard me and jogged across. 'What happened? Why are you here?'

'Nothing happened.' My dad had gone to bed happy, I'd lain awake wondering what to do next. 'Listen, I need you to remember Rupert Ecclestone's New York number.'

Instead of asking more questions, Carter dropped his head and stood with a frown of concentration. He came out with '212 717 6669.' Just like that.

'Thanks.' I knew I could rely on him for this kind of stuff.

Across the court, Mel blew his whistle to re-start the session.

212 717 6669. I punched in the numbers and waited, with Connie and Zoey hovering beside me.

It was lunchtime Thursday and they'd come to my house to offer me advice.

'Call the number!' Connie had insisted. 'Make out that you want to buy some serious art!'

So I was expecting a secretary's voice saying something like, 'Nicholsons Fine Art, how may I help you?'

Zoey and Connie had planned my reply. 'Hi there, I'd like to speak with Rupert Ecclestone, please.' Real casual and sounding young and happening, with loads of dough behind me. Someone who might be interested in spending a few hundred thousand of Daddy's dollars on oil-paint and canvas.

But what I got was a low-key recorded message. 'Hi. There's no one home to take your call . . .'

I frowned and put down the phone. 'That must be his apartment number. Elizabeth obviously calls him out of office hours.'

We sat around for a while until Zoey got us out of what felt like a blind alley. 'Call your mom in New York instead, ask her to check stuff out,' she suggested. 'I'd place a lot of money on her being able to help!'

'Hi, Mom, it's me.'

'Kate, honey. Listen, I have two clients in the gallery so make this quick, OK?'

Mommy dearest. 'Here's a name,' I told her. No explanations necessary. 'It's a guy called Rupert Ecclestone, who allegedly works for Nicholsons as Elizabeth Grant's boss . . .'

'OK, got it!' Mom said. 'Leave it with me.'

Click. The line went dead.

Five minutes later, Connie, Zoey and me were halfway through making toasted cheese sandwiches for lunch when Mom called back.

'Hi, honey. Get this. Rupert Ecclestone did work for Nicholsons in Sloane Square in London. But he lost his position with them five weeks back.'

'Did they dismiss him?' This was getting more interesting by the minute.

'Nobody actually admits it because it's bad for business. But yeah, according to my inside contacts, they had to get rid of him.'

'Because?' I sensed that Mom was holding back with the killer punch as a kind of tease. In other

64

words, she was enjoying delivering the news.

'Something to do with concealing stolen art treasures. Rembrandts, Turners, some French Impressionists. Or maybe not stolen exactly, but looted from European museums way back during the Second World War. I mean, we're talking fifty years ago, and it's only lately that some of these looted treasures have been traced.'

Mom was in full swing now. 'There's activity at the level of national governments to get this stuff returned to the rightful owners, but a lot of it is still slipping through the official net. According to my source, it looks like your Rupert Ecclestone was part of a network that's trying to secretly shift the more valuable items in London from out of museum vaults into private collections. Nothing was proved, but there was enough suspicion to make it possible for the company to dismiss him.'

'And now he's over here and in contact with Elizabeth,' I told her.

'Plus she's lying about her employers.' Mom laid it on thick. 'Kate, honey, how come your father is such a sad, gullible schmuck as to believe in this woman?'

'Mom, cut it out. Thanks for doing what you did, but will you give me the space to handle it this end, please?'

There was a short pause, then a loud sigh. 'OK, Kate. But take my advice: don't wait too long to tell your father that Elizabeth Grant is a crook.'

'*May be* a crook!' I insisted. 'Isn't there something about being innocent until proved guilty? Anyhow, what's the problem with taking it slowly and letting him down gently?'

Mom's answer went some way to proving that deep down in that materialistic, manipulative heart of hers, she still did care a little about my dad.

'Because the longer you leave it, the more involved Sean's gonna get and the harder he's gonna fall!'

Give Connie and Zoey a chance, and they're into detection work big time.

I mean, until now it's always been me and Carter. But since he was too busy playing basketball, they stepped right into his shoes.

'What have we got so far?' Zoey said, spreading one hand and checking items off finger by finger. 'A, we got the fact that Elizabeth Grant has invented a job which she doesn't have. B, she's hooked up with some guy involved in a crooked supply of stolen art works to private collectors who don't ask too many questions about the source and provenance of the latest masterpiece on offer.'

'Source and what?' Connie quizzed. She was looking at fluffy little Zoey with new respect.

'Provenance – history – who last owned the picture, that kind of stuff.' Zoey pressed on to the third finger. 'C, she has two British passports, one of which definitely belongs to someone else.'

This is where I got a word in. 'Yeah, listen we need to know more about this Sara Hyde Smith.'

'If she exists,' Connie said.

'Sure she does. She's on this list of ex-students.' I held up the crumpled sheet of paper which I'd firmly held on to since my visit to Cyberama with Carter.

Zoey pounced on it. 'There's a contact number here!' she cried. 'C'mon, Kate, call it for Chrissake!'

'What am I gonna say?' I demanded, as Connie pressed the keypad on the telephone and brought up the international code for England.

'You'll think of something!' she told me. 'Tell the woman you're Sara Hyde Smith's illegitimate daughter, adopted by rich Texas oil barons but desperate to get in contact with your birth mother.'

I glowered at her as I caught the phone.

'506123.' A woman spoke. She sounded uncannily like Elizabeth; the same classy accent, the same confidence. 'Claire Bousanquet speaking.'

'Mrs Bousanquet, my name's Kate Brennan . . .'

('Doh!' I heard both Connie and Zoey groan at me behind my back for giving her my real name. OK, so that was a mistake.)

'I'm a research student at Yale University, working for my masters thesis on the decline of the English public school system during the nineteen-seventies through to the end of the millennium.'

('Wow!' Gasps of admiration this time from my noisy associates.)

'As a follow-up appendix, I need to list the current professions of students whose names are listed as alumni on the Bath Ladies College website. Of course, such information will be treated as entirely confidential.' I paused and waited for a response.

'Might your thesis allow for the fact that the English public school system is still very much alive and well in the twenty-first century?' Claire Bousanquet asked. 'Far from being in decline, schools such as Bath are in fact as popular as they ever were.'

'Of course,' I agreed, giving Zoey and Connie a thumbs-up signal. The fish had bitten. 'Which is why I need to take certain names at random and feed the information you give me about their careers into my statistical analysis. Take the year of Elizabeth Grant, for instance. This just a name taken off the available list of ex-students. How many girls in her class later practiced medicine or law, say?'

'Oh, Elizabeth! She was in the year above me as a matter of fact.' Claire had decided I was genuine, and she was a lady with no brakes on her thought processes. She relaxed into co-operative, motormouth mode. 'All the girls looked up to her; she was our role model, you might say.'

'And what career did she follow?'

The question drew a hollow laugh from Mrs Bousanquet. 'Ah now, there you go, choosing precisely the wrong name on the list!'

'How come?'

'Elizabeth is one of the few – the very few – Bath Ladies College girls whose later careers we don't care to talk about.'

'Really?' I tried not to sound too interested, but it was difficult. 'How come exactly?'

'It's sad really. As I said, we all looked up to Elizabeth. But it turned out that she did nothing with her talents. No, she chose the old-fashioned, pre-feminist thing of marrying well at the age of nineteen. He was the second son of a marquis, dabbling in the world of antiques and fine art.'

'He was? That doesn't sound like too bad a career move,' I commented. Some might even say her future looked bright at this point.

'Except that her husband soon managed to blow his part of the family fortune on other women and an out of control drugs habit,' Claire confided. 'Cocaine mostly. He bankrupted himself and ended up in jail.'

'You could hardly blame Elizabeth for what happened to her husband?' I pointed out.

(Connie and Zoey stared open-mouthed when I mentioned the word 'husband' in connection with Elizabeth. Luckily, they didn't make too much noise this time, apart from the odd squeak of disbelief.)

'That would normally be true, I agree. But there had been a lot of scandal in the tabloids and society pages about Elizabeth's extravagant lifestyle. Friends of her husband, Alex, claimed that she pushed him into addiction with her high living, and even that she pushed him into the arms of other women, like Sara, for example.'

'Sara?' By now the effort to keep up my research student front was beginning to show.

'Another sad story,' Claire confessed. 'Sara Hyde Smith and Elizabeth had been best friends all the time they were at the College. It was one of those inseparable friendships, and odd because the two girls were born on the same day, and they even looked quite alike. Both tall and fabulous looking, with small, pretty features and identical styles. It was if they were twins in every sense except the genetic one.'

Mrs Bousanquet loaded this story with a tone of deep regret which I was itching to get to the bottom of. 'But the friendship went wrong in the end?'

She sighed loudly. 'Yes. You remember that famous quote from Princess Diana about her relationship with Prince Charles? She said, "There were three people in this marriage," meaning Camilla. Well, it was the same with Alex, Elizabeth and Sara. The situation had gone on in secret for years. But Elizabeth finally discovered the truth after Alex had been sent to prison. And of course, that was the end of a beautiful friendship.'

'And end of story?' I prompted, sensing that no, not quite. There was more to come.

'If only!' Claire Bousanquet seemed to have forgotten the official purpose of my phone call and was dishing the dirt on her ex-school buddies with tabloid fervour. 'Poor Sara stuck with Alex even in his darkest days, while Elizabeth promptly and publicly divorced him. She reverted to her maiden name of Grant and struck out ambitiously in the world of fine art, making quite a name for herself and building up links with some of the best dealers in London: Sothebys, Nicholsons and so on . . .'

'So why "poor Sara"?' I asked. It sounded to me like she'd made some pretty dumb choices back there.

'One has to feel sorry . . .' For the first time, Mrs Motormouth hesitated. At this point it was obvious that she felt she might be dragging the name of her precious school through the dirt. But then, hey, everyone knew the gory details already. I guess that was how she justified passing on this final piece of information.

'Sara paid the price of being involved with Alex Monkman's world,' she told me. 'Just last month. It was all over the newspapers; a very high profile case. The police are convinced that there's a drugs underworld connection, but so far there have been no definite leads.'

'When you say she paid the price, what happened exactly?' I asked. I was hardly able to stop Connie and Zoey from tearing the phone out of my hands, they were so eager to hear the news.

'Murder,' Mrs Bousanquet told us. 'Poor Sara was found dead in her mews house just off Russell Square,

72

Central London. She'd been shot twice through the head.'

6

Pay attention, because things move fast from here on in. They caught me off guard, when my head was full of the big ball game I'd fixed up to see with Ziggy.

We'd spent Thursday morning at the coaching session, then mooched around my place all afternoon. Zig said Zoey was busy with Connie and Kate – 'les girls' – so why didn't we hang around in my basement? Ditto all day Friday. The girls were busy and Zig and me were surplus to requirements.

I admit to a minuscule level of jealousy here. OK, so Kate often got together with Zoey and Connie, but how come she'd made a point of asking me for this Rupert guy's phone number if she didn't plan to involve me in future developments? I mean, that could look like exploiting me for my fabulous photographic memory or something.

Anyhow, it felt like Kate was cutting me out, and this was me getting my own back by sulking.

So I made my point by not showing up at her place

until Friday evening. And I'd already filled up Saturday with a bus journey to the stadium and the game itself. This was me saying to Kate, 'You can stick your Elizabeth Grant mystery wherever you want.'

Only, I couldn't stay away from Constitution Square for more than forty-eight hours, which is why I ended up at Kate's house early Friday evening.

And I found Connie hanging around outside the bookstore opposite.

'Hey,' I said as I walked by.

'Ssh!' Connie hissed.

I shot a look over my shoulder. 'How come, "Ssh!"?'

'Carter, quit it. You're drawing attention to me!'

Which was a joke. I mean, Connie's blonde halo, her nose-studs, eyebrow rings and stuff make a pretty loud statement all on their own. Passers-by stare at Connie, which is the effect she aims for.

'What are you doing?' I asked.

'I'm tailing Elizabeth Grant,' she muttered, her attention fixed on the door to number 18. 'She came out of work, caught the train up here, and she's in there now.'

'So?' This information put me off my stride. I didn't look forward to running into Ms Grant after the passport fiasco. I mean, what if Dragon-Secretary Monica had caught a glimpse and recognised me even beneath my courier's helmet? Maybe this was the reason why Elizabeth had paid Sean a visit. Or else it could be romantic candlelit dinner chez Sean number two. Who could tell?

'So, it's bad news,' Connie told me darkly. 'The woman's dangerous, Carter. We've gotta stop her.'

'From doing what?' I leaned against the bookstore window until the owner rapped on the pane and told me to shift my butt.

'We don't know yet. But we gotta stop her.' Connie's mouth went tight and button-shaped. No way was she gonna spill the beans to mere me.

'Yeah, like she's a mad axe-murderer!' I snorted.

'That's not funny, Carter!' Con practically bit my head off. 'There's one woman dead already in this whole big mess!'

Like I say, this caught me off-guard. 'Who's dead?'

'Sara Hyde Smith. She was killed in London last month. A professional hit – two bullets in the brain.'

It took five minutes for Connie to bring me up to speed. Stuff about aristocratic families, marriages, affairs – oh, and drugs. 'So the British cops put it down to an underworld assassination?' I checked.

'Yeah, but Zoey and me have another theory.' By this time Connie had dropped the inscrutable act and was gabbling fast. 'We think Elizabeth had the job done because she was crazy over the affair Sara had with her lousy, no-good husband. She just made it look like a drugs-related crime.'

'So what's your evidence?' I was back to scoffing and snorting. Like, this was Connie's imagination running wild.

'The passport!' she declared.

This was the moment the bookstore guy chose to rap the window, making me almost jump out of my skin.

Connie thought she'd stunned me with her brilliance. 'How else would Elizabeth Grant be in possession of a murdered woman's passport unless she'd stolen it from her room after she'd shot her through the head?'

Well, no time to think that one through. What happened next was that the door to Kate's house opened and Elizabeth and Kate appeared on the stoop. It was obvious that there was a big fight going on.

As Connie darted into the bookstore to avoid being seen, I got it into my head that I needed to break up the fight. So I strode across the square.

When I say fight, I mean a lot of loud arguing between Kate and Elizabeth. Not physical contact.

'You can defend your precious boyfriend all you like,'

Elizabeth told her as I came within earshot. 'But I'm telling your father that Joey Carter is a bad influence, and he ought to put a stop to you seeing him!'

'I'm not seeing him!' Steam practically came out of Kate's ears as she yelled back. 'Carter's not my boyfriend!'

This boosted my ego to gigantic proportions – not. In fact, I almost sidestepped out of sight, but Sean came to the door behind Kate and spotted me.

'Hold it, Joey!' he called.

No chance of me making a run for it, then. So I reluctantly climbed the stoop and went inside the house.

'Elizabeth's been making some pretty serious allegations,' Sean warned me. We stood in the wide hallway, everyone looking like someone had put firecrackers under our feet.

'Yeah, and they're not true!' Kate insisted. 'Carter, she's claiming you stole a portfolio of valuable drawings from off of her desk!'

I nearly fell over. Then I recovered. 'So call the cops,' I told Elizabeth calmly. 'Go ahead, do it.'

She met me eyeball to eyeball. 'Let's stick to the facts,' she replied. Ironic, huh? 'What I've told Sean is that you played a trick on my secretary to divert her attention . . .'

Sean jumped in with, 'Did you, Joey?'

He was a hard guy to lie to, so I blushed and nodded.

'And while she was away, you took the opportunity to slip a couple of small preliminary sketches from the portfolio – by a minor nineteenth-century artist, as it turns out.'

'No way!' Why did I sound so pathetic and Elizabeth so convincing? I reckon it's all down to the accent. But then that's the giant chip on my shoulder.

Kate charged to my support. 'Like I said, Dad, we did have a reason to visit Elizabeth at her office . . .'

'Which you can't explain,' he reminded her. Sean was looking confused and disappointed. 'Or which you refuse to tell me about . . .'

Elizabeth's turn to interrupt. 'You didn't think for a moment I would fall for that story about you being interested in the Impressionists,' she scoffed at me. 'Maybe you can wrap Kate round your little finger and persuade her to believe any kind of nonsense you tell her. You can set up a situation just so you can scout around in a place where there are bound to be valuable paintings, but don't imagine you can fool anybody else with that butter-wouldn't-melt image.'

'So go ahead, call the cops.' I called her bluff a second time.

'Oh this is so stupid!' Kate turned to her dad with the palms of both hands stretched towards him. 'Can't you see she's making this up? You know Joey wouldn't do anything like that!'

Elizabeth just sighed, clasped her hands in front of her and looked heavenwards. Martyr pose.

'Why would Elizabeth lie?' was Sean's question.

Neither of us could explain. All we had on his girlfriend was an unhappy ex-marriage and a dead woman's passport. Plus a dubious artworld connection and little economy with the truth about her job.

'You just have to believe us!' Kate cried. 'Please, Dad.'

He gazed at us, one at a time. Finally his eyes came to rest on Elizabeth, still looking like a study for Joan of Arc. 'Thank you,' he said softly. 'I know this can't have been easy for you.'

'Thank you for what?' Kate yelled, coming to stand alongside me. 'Thank you for screwing up our lives? Thank you for lying about the best friend I have in the whole world?'

I almost fell over a second time, I was so stunned by this.

Sean turned sadly towards us. 'I'm thanking Elizabeth for not going to the cops and instead coming here to give you a second chance,' he said quietly.

This was an example of a man believing that the sun shines out of the top of his lover's head. They talk about falling in love, being enslaved, driven crazy, out of touch with reality. And it all turns out to be true.

It made Kate turn her back with tears of frustration. She rushed for the door, with me close behind.

'Kate!' Sean called her back. He didn't want it to end this way. But he didn't make a move to follow us either. He just stood with Elizabeth in the hallway.

She ignored him and ran into the street.

'What happened?' Connie flew out of the bookstore doorway and met us in the middle of the Square.

Kate sobbed and let Connie put her arms round her. 'Look at what she did now!' she wailed, hands over her eyes, hiding her face against Connie's shoulder. 'She's driving Dad away from me with her lies. Connie, I can't bear it if that happens. You've gotta help straighten this out, please!'

The big problem was, no way did Elizabeth Grant look like a person who'd been touched by evil.

You expect an outward sign: a twisted face, mean eyes, a cruel mouth.

But Elizabeth had the looks of a saint: clear grey eyes, almost invisible eyebrows, a high, smooth forehead and that silky curtain of golden hair.

Appearances in this case were deceptive, though. And

at this point on Friday evening I didn't voice any objection when Connie introduced the notion of evil and said that Elizabeth Grant was in the grip of some wicked, unseen force.

'We have to stop her!' Connie insisted. She's a warrior-woman when she wants to be. Fearless, with no room in her head for doubt.

'Yeah, but we need to be smart.' I pointed out that it was an intelligent move on Elizabeth's part to drive a wedge between Kate and Sean before we had a chance to gather enough evidence to turn him against her. It meant she'd reacted to us snooping around her office with a pre-emptive strike. Get in there before the enemy does.

'OK, so we need to work out exactly what she has going in the art underworld,' Connie decided.

All this time, we were tucked away behind the bookshelves in the late night bookstore and Kate was busy trying not to cry. She was having a hard time getting over the fight with Sean.

'We're thinking big-time looting of treasures from European museums,' Connie continued.

Mister Bookstore Man stood behind his cash desk and stared at us over the top of his glasses like we were three crazies escaped from the asylum.

'Keep your voice down!' I warned Con.

She took no notice. 'These mega-valuable items have been stashed away in vaults for half a century. Then suddenly, some organisation gets working to restore the stuff looted by the Nazis in the 1940s to their rightful owners. The men in the museums panic at having to own up to what they're keeping hidden in their basements. This is when one or two shady art dealers seize their chance . . .'

'*Puh-lease!*' The bookstore guy sighed and tutted. Like, which James Bond movie had we been to see lately?

Connie crushed him with a scornful glance. 'Art dealers like this Rupert Ecclestone and dear Elizabeth,' she went on, 'they know the millionaires of this world who were born minus scruples. That is, these guys will trample over any law to get what they want.'

'Which is *all* millionaires,' Kate said quietly.

So I knew she was getting over her trauma.

'So Elizabeth and Rupert build up contacts who will pay mega-bucks to acquire art which was basically stolen by the Nazis a couple of generations back. And they steal them all over again, to order, with the co-operation of some of these crooked museum guys.'

'Yeah, right!' Kate agreed with Connie's theory.

Privately, I wished I'd worked this out for myself, then

it would be me who Kate was admiring.

'Listen!' The guy who owned the store came out from behind his desk. He'd taken off his silver-rimmed glasses and was swinging them by one arm as he advanced towards us. 'Unless you three plan to purchase the latest annotated edition of Dostoevski's *Crime and Punishment* or the illustrated version of *The Compleat Angler*, would you please leave the premises!'

So we were lurking with intent in the Square when Elizabeth Grant came out of Number 18. We watched her wave to Sean and step into a taxi, quickly found ourselves one and ordered the driver to, yeah, 'Follow that cab!'

It wasn't so much taking corners on two wheels and squeals of tyres on tarmac as jerking, stop-start through the Friday evening traffic heading for a night out in town. Eventually we reached State Hill and watched Elizabeth stop her cab and step out on to the sidewalk outside the most expensive restaurant in town. French, of course.

We got out fifty yards up the street, paid our driver and hung around suspiciously as Elizabeth entered 'L'Echiquier'.

Chauffeur-driven women in stretch limousines glared at us as they cruised down the dark, glittering street. Hotel doormen got ready to call the cops. I mean, what were three kids like us doing loitering at the corner of the most expensive block of real estate outside of Manhattan?

We waited two hours in the January cold. Customers came and went from the restaurant, but Elizabeth took her time over the nouvelle cuisine. Finally, though, she did emerge.

The doorman held the door and she stepped out with two guys. A car jockey drove a big Mercedes alongside, the three people shook hands in a businesslike way, and one guy (tall, overweight, flashy) took over the Mercedes driving-seat. He soon cruised away down the street.

Elizabeth and the remaining guy watched him leave with smiles and waves. They looked happy and relaxed with the way the meal had gone. Elizabeth linked arms with the second guy (also tall, but slim and good-looking in an understated, classy way). She spoke excitedly, tossed her hair back behind her shoulder, gave the guy a kiss on the cheek. Extra-friendly. Then they walked off arm in arm.

I felt Kate stiffen at the realisation that Sean wasn't the only star twinkling on Elizabeth Grant's romantic horizon. And before I could stop her, I saw Connie walk on up to the doorman before Elizabeth and her guy had turned the corner.

Put this down to Connie's inexperience. Also the fact that she's impatient by nature. Anyway, when Elizabeth did reach the end of the block and turn to glance back the way she'd walked, Connie was already deep in conversation with the doorman and me and Kate were hovering in the background. So she definitely saw all three of us before she and Mr Elegant finally turned off.

Meanwhile, Connie was asking the man in uniform an inspired question. A long shot, maybe, but one that paid off. 'Which one of those two guys was Rupert Ecclestone?'

'Who wants to know?' came the suspicious reply.

'I do. I have a small package for him. He called my employer to have it delivered to him at the restaurant, but it looks like I just missed him.'

The doorman's brain wouldn't get him into Mensa. A more alert guy would've asked, 'How come you know you got the correct party?' or 'Didn't your boss provide a description of Ecclestone for you to work with?' But no. He shrugged like it didn't matter, and what did he care? 'Ecclestone's the guy with the dame,' he told us.

'Not the guy in the Mercedes?' Connie pressed. She sure pushed her luck.

'Nope. That's Maurice Brown. Everyone knows him. He just bought half of the Hollywood film industry. Steven Spielberg, watch your ass!'

7

I pushed Dad's glass of OJ across the breakfast bar in the kitchen.

He took it without looking up from his newspaper.

That felt like someone had stabbed me in the stomach; just the fact that he didn't look up and say thanks.

It's the small things that get to you.

I spent the whole of Saturday morning on chores around the house, hoping that things would get back to normal, with a feeling inside that I could easily bleed to death unless we did something to heal the wound.

I mean, my dad and I are close. *Were* close; before Elizabeth Grant showed up and twisted everything up between us.

'What's your schedule for the day?' I asked him over lunch. Neither of us had eaten much of the pizza I'd bought in from The Four Seasons across the Square.

'No plans for today,' he muttered. Then, 'I invited

Elizabeth round tomorrow evening.'

Great! Fine! Add anger to the hurt I was feeling, and you have a pretty explosive mix. I stormed out to the hallway to answer the phone.

'Hey, Kate,' Zoey said. Her voice had a nervous edge.

'Hey, Zoey. What's wrong?'

'Is Connie at your place by any chance?'

'Nope. Haven't seen her since last evening.' I recalled the look of triumph on her face when she'd identified Rupert Ecclestone as Elizabeth's dinner companion. But to be honest, since we'd split off and gone our separate ways home soon after, I hadn't given anyone except my dad too much thought. 'Why? Did you lose her?'

'Yeah. She was supposed to meet up with me. We planned to visit a couple of department stores while Joey and Zig went to the ball game. Only she didn't show up.'

'Oh, you know how Con is,' I said in an offhand way.

'Exactly!' Zoey pulled me up short. 'When did you ever know Connie not to show up when she promised?'

Connie may look scary and offbeat, but you can set

your wristwatch by her. She has method behind her madness, if you know what I mean. So, yeah, this was slightly worrying.

Even more so when Zoey explained Connie's movements for the morning just gone by. 'Guess what that crazy girl had in mind?' she told me. 'Something about riding the train over to East Grand Street to stake out number 428.'

'Who lives there?' I asked. My own strung out nerves were beginning to jump like crazy.

'Some Rupert Ecclestone guy.'

My stomach did a somersault and threatened to re-present me with the small slice of pizza I'd just eaten. 'How does she know that?'

'You know Con,' Zoey said back at me. 'She got it into her head that she'd find out where this guy stayed. So she went over to some French restaurant on State Hill and worked on a manager there to divulge the information. Try saying no to Connie when she's in that kind of mood.'

'Pity the poor guy,' I said, unsuccessfully trying to lighten things. 'How do you know all this?'

'Because she called me to put back the time for us to meet. Said she was going to check out 428 East Grand Street before she met me at 1.30.'

I looked at the clock on the wall. It said 1.45. 'Maybe she got held up in traffic.'

Zoey sighed. 'She'd have called to say she was gonna be late.'

'Only fifteen minutes behind schedule,' I pointed out.

'Kate,' Zoey protested. 'I'm worried about her.'

I took a deep breath and tried not to let my imagination run riot. 'Me too,' I admitted. It looked like Connie had done her thing of rushing in headlong again. 'Majorly worried. If she doesn't show up soon, I think we should call the cops.'

Twenty-four hours later, Connie was officially missing.

Dad and I had visited her place to speak with her mom and dad and I told the cops everything I knew. Which was that Connie had set out for East Grand Street and hadn't been seen since.

Connie's mom, Shawna, came at me with a storm of questions – apparently the same ones she'd already asked Zoey. How come Connie was in that part of town? Who did she know in East Village? What had this Rupert Ecclestone guy got to do with anything?

Zoey, Zig, Carter and me always referred to Shawna Oseles as 'The Explanation'. Meet her mother, and you understand everything about Connie – how come she's so headstrong and individualistic, why she loves people to look at her, and the reason she never sticks to the rules. Undiluted seventies feminism is Shawna's thing; all men are equal, but women are more equal than others. And man, does she let you know it.

Yet now that her daughter was missing, Shawna acted pretty much like any other mother, firing off the questions in a desperate effort to solve the mystery.

It was one of the cops who slowed her down. 'Excuse me, ma'am, do you mind if I ask Kate a few questions myself?'

A deliberate, heavy-set guy in uniform, he sat me down on the Oseleses' sofa and quietly grilled me.

'Kate, can you tell us what you know about Rupert Ecclestone?'

'Not a whole lot,' I confessed. It was uncomfortable to have Dad sitting in on this because it would soon become obvious to him that I'd been snooping around on Elizabeth's territory. I felt him grow more still and stiff, the way he does when the tension of a situation gets through to him. 'I know via my mom that he worked at one time for Nicholsons Fine Art Dealers in London. He lost that job about five weeks back, but Joey Carter and I found out that Elizabeth Grant, who is a friend of my father's, is still in contact with him over here in Fortune City.'

The methodical cop jotted down some details, then nodded at me to continue.

'That's it.' I shrugged and stared at the rug.

'What kind of contact does Elizabeth Grant have with Ecclestone?' the sergeant asked. 'Is it business or social?'

'Both.' I swallowed hard and told him what Connie, Carter and I had witnessed outside the restaurant on Friday night.

Dad went rigid. I thought he'd stopped breathing. And he was ghostly white, poor guy.

'Listen, why don't you ask Rupert Ecclestone about his relationship with Elizabeth?' I pleaded.

The cop flipped his notepad shut and stuck it in his shirt pocket. 'We already tried,' he informed us. 'I sent a guy over to East Grand Street, but the place was locked up – nobody home.'

Nightmare. Connie was missing and Ecclestone had most likely got her. You didn't need to be Einstein.

Plus, Dad's world had collapsed, and it felt like my fault.

I hadn't even told him the truth, the whole truth

and nothing but the truth, yet either. So when we left the Oseleses in bits and arrived back at Constitution Square, I had to work out, do I break it to him gently, or do I dive in with our suspicions about the dead woman in the London apartment and her passport on Elizabeth's desk?

. . . 'We're talking murder here?' Dad stammered.

I'd gone for the second option, on the basis that you have to be cruel to be kind. But then I realised I'd taken him a step too far.

He stood up from the kitchen table. 'You're crazy! Elizabeth?' He sat down again with a sudden jolt. 'There's no evidence, is there?'

'Only the passport,' I reminded him. Even to me, it seemed a pretty slim connection. 'But she's definitely mixed up with Ecclestone, and there's plenty of people with serious doubts about that guy.' I'd told the police all this, and said that Joey Carter could confirm it.

Dad closed his eyes and leaned heavily on the table. 'Have I been a total schmuck?' he whispered.

I waited a while. 'Elizabeth puts on a pretty good act. She could fool most guys.'

'You look at her and you think, wow, am I dreaming? She has class, she's smart, witty . . .'

'. . . English?' I suggested.

He raised a half-smile. 'Yeah, that too. I thought, how come a woman like that is interested in me?'

I told him he was too modest. 'Any woman in the world would fall for you in a big way; you need to remember that!' I meant it then and I still do.

'So why was Elizabeth using the internet to find guys to date?' Dad was beginning to use his brain at last. 'Was it because she advertised herself in a way that would appeal to guys with plenty of dough?'

I agreed with this. 'She uses Kismet as a short cut to meeting wealthy contacts. She lets men wine and dine her and then she moves in with the spiel about a special painting that has just come on the market. Nobody knows it's for sale except Elizabeth, Ecclestone and a few important contacts. Hence it can be bought for less than it would fetch at public auction . . . the guy bites. Elizabeth makes a sale, travels back to Europe on a dead woman's passport so that her movements can't be traced . . .'

Dad got the picture. (Sorry about the wordplay.) 'She arrives in London, Paris, Munich, wherever. She does the deal and couriers the painting back to the States. The buyer gets his looted masterpiece, puts it in a frame and hangs it to gloat over where no one can see it. The money is shared out between the crooked museum guy, Ecclestone and Elizabeth. Everybody's happy.'

'Except the genuine owners snarled up in a long legal battle in the European courts to get their property back.' The crooks had it all sewn up real neat. And we were talking a scam worth millions of dollars. But I could see that Dad had had enough. I put my hand over his. 'Sorry,' I whispered.

He shook his head. 'So what happened to Connie? Did she get careless and let Ecclestone see she was spying on him?'

'I guess.' Invisibility wasn't her strong point. And she was new to the undercover stuff.

'So she's in danger?'

I nodded.

'How much danger?'

'Who knows?' A lot, when you thought about it.

I mean, what do major league criminals do when amateurs tread on their toes? They don't just beat them up and toss them back on the street. They fix them for good.

8

The reason I was hiding alone in a phone booth in East Park Avenue late Sunday afternoon was complicated.

After two hours I was freezing cold in the wind and hail. I'd been moved on twice by the traffic cops and was wishing for sure that I'd never even heard the name Elizabeth Grant.

So why East Park Avenue? Hold it; let me go back to breakfast time, which is when I first heard that Connie was missing. Official.

'The cops are round at the Oseleses' place,' Zig informed me when he showed up on my doorstep and hauled me out of bed. He and I had arrived back late from the ball game the night before, which is the reason I was out of touch with Kate and also why I'd slept late. But by 9 am Zig was already live and kicking. 'Zoey had to go down to Precinct Headquarters to tell them everything she knew. Carter, wake up, this is a big deal!'

Fern and Damien had let Ziggy in the house, then

enjoyed jumping on my head to bring me out of a deep sleep.

'How can Connie be missing?' I mumbled, stumbling out of bed and poking my head through the neck of a T-shirt I'd left lying on the floor. 'I just saw her Friday night.'

'It happened yesterday. Zoey thinks maybe she stuck her nose in where it wasn't safe; like, she only went to stake out Rupert Ecclestone's place!'

He filled me in as I climbed into a pair of jeans, splashed cold water over my face and showed my teeth a toothbrush. 'Not very smart of her,' I muttered. Especially since I was pretty sure that Elizabeth Grant and Ecclestone had already noted Connie in animated conversation with the guy on the door at L'Echiquier. 'What are the cops doing?'

Ziggy shrugged. 'Mel's not on the case. But what he gets on the grapevine down the Precinct is that they're securing a warrant to break open Ecclestone's apartment and take a look around. They think that's their best lead.'

By this time, my brain was in overdrive. 'Will they pick up Elizabeth Grant for questioning?'

He shook his head. 'They don't see any reason why she should be involved in Connie's disappearance.'

'Huh.' Ms Squeaky-Clean. But you could understand why the cops would leave her out of the picture; she just didn't look the evil type, like I said already. 'What about Maurice Brown?'

(Which is where the new Mr Big of Hollywood comes into it, and his address on East Park Avenue. And how come I'm shivering inside the phone booth. So stick around a while longer.)

'Never heard of him,' Ziggy grunted.

Which meant that the multi-millionaire wasn't in the official frame either. But I'd had an unofficial feeling about him ever since I saw him outside the restaurant on Friday night.

I pictured him again: Mr Smug, Mr Cheesy. Thousands of dollars worth of tailored cloth draped over his well-fed bulk. Rolex probably told him the time and Aspreys put the diamond in his gold ear-stud. Not that I have a thing against men with mega-bucks – really! No, it had been his fat, cheesy smile and the way he'd totally ignored the car jockey when he elbowed him out of the way and jumped into the Mercedes that got under my skin.

And Maurice Brown had been the name Elizabeth had mentioned when we were in her office. She'd scuttled off to see him and his money, remember. So to me it looked like Brown was a big player in their looted paintings scam; either a major buyer or part of the actual organisation.

'Do you know where Kate is now?' I asked Zig.

'She's talking to the cops over at the Oseleses' place. Why?'

'Never mind. There's something I want to do.' Like, find out more about Maurice Brown via Angel Christian, who was Sean Brennan's boss and the only person I knew in Fortune City who was rich enough to move in the same circles as Movie Mogul Maurice.

Ziggy went off to meet up with Zoey and I called Angel on my cell-phone. I'd hit the street and was heading for the train station.

'Maurice Brown is not on my Christmas card list,' Angel told me when I got past her Rottweiler-style housekeeper. She launched right into why she didn't like the guy. 'He's a back-stabbing megalomaniac with an ego the size of the Empire State Building. Also, he married a girlfriend of mine, humiliated her when they were together and threw her out with the garbage once he'd lined up wife number four.'

Ouch! 'Could he also be into buying up stolen masterpieces?' I asked, real casual.

Angel laughed. 'Oh yeah. The guy has a private gallery the length of a football field at his place on East Park Avenue. He collects art like other people collect supermarket vouchers. And Brown never considers the small matter of ethics in any of his other business ventures, so why should he even ask where a painting or a statue came from? If he wants it, he gets it.'

'This house on East Park Avenue; does it have big security systems in place?'

'Yeah, Joey.' Angel laughed again. 'Why?'

'No reason.'

'You're not thinking of turning art thief?'

'No. I'm looking for a friend,' I told her. End of conversation. I thanked Angel for Maurice Brown's address, clicked off the phone and jumped on the train.

So, two hours later I'm checking out the mansion from the phone booth and losing my enthusiasm fast.

A hunch is no protection against a freezing temperature and an empty stretch of pure boredom, broken only by a couple of suspicious traffic cops with nothing better to do than move me on.

So I called Kate.

'Carter, that sounds like a long shot,' she told me after I'd explained my sub-arctic mission.

'Yeah, I kn-n-n-ow!' My teeth chattered; my jaw was rigid with cold. 'And the only thing I've seen come through the gates of Brown's place is a ground-squirrel and a magpie.'

'One for sorrow.' She quoted me the start of the old rhyme. Two for joy, three for a girl . . .

'Th-h-h-hanks! Why don't you join me?' Now, there was an attractive proposition for a guy like me to make to a girl like Kate.

'And freeze to death? No listen, I'm back at my place with Dad. He's expecting Elizabeth to show up any time now and I want to be here when she does.' Kate gave a good reason for leaving me to my solo mission. 'Do you really think Brown could be implicated in Connie's disappearance?' she wanted to know.

'He's in the p-p-picture somewhere,' I insisted. While the cops were checking out Rupert Ecclestone, and Kate and Sean were trying to squeeze some information out of Elizabeth Grant, I still reckoned my best bet was East Park Avenue.

'OK, so keep in touch.' She signed off briskly, as if things had started moving at her end. 'Gotta go, Carter; bye!'

And she left me wishing for an event on the Avenue that would take my mind off the size of the hailstones.

I counted the number of silver cars passing by. Then the red ones. I'd reached a mind-numbing count of cars with alloy wheels when finally a florist's delivery van approached the gates to 165.

165 East Park Avenue may not sound like a big deal, so I'd better fill in the picture. Don't think 'house', think 'mansion', maybe even 'shopping mall'. Brown's place is huge, set in a park all of its own. The building is state-of-the-art architecture; square with lots of extra wings and extensions. There's a dome of glass and steel topping the whole thing which is what reminds me of the mall, but then my taste in modern buildings isn't reliable.

Anyway, the Jacaranda flower van was caught on the security camera poised on the gate-post. It gained admittance. The gates swung open by remote control and in it went, up the drive with snowy lawns to either side, until it crunched to a halt outside what looked like a service entrance to the side of the main building.

So what? Lilies and roses got delivered by the truck-load to houses like this. I read that Elton John spends thousands of dollars a day on flowers. But today was Sunday, and even florists to the mega-rich get weekends off. So I took a second look at the Jacaranda driver – and that was when my interest suddenly sparked.

A small woman dressed in a bright orange, padded jacket stepped out of the van. The orange clashed with her short red hair. I noticed the eyeglasses, then I registered the identity – Monica! How come Elizabeth Grant's secretary was moonlighting as a flower delivery driver?

And how come she left the back doors of the van open and went to the door for help to carry the delivery into the house? Surely flowers didn't weigh too much for one person to carry?

By this time I'd left my phone booth, crossed the road and was peering through the bars of the high iron railings. I saw Maurice Brown himself answer the service door. Didn't the guy have half a dozen housekeepers to do that for him? This was weird, and got weirder.

Brown listened to Monica, who looked stressed out. He nodded and came out into the yard. Together they leaned into the back of the van and pulled hard at a long, heavy object roughly wrapped in the kind of plastic bubble-wrap you get around packages.

No way were these gerbera for the dining-table. The thing weighed a ton as they dragged it into view. Then Brown shoved Monica to one side, took the weight of it in both arms and carried it into the house.

Now I was really worried.

I mean, that bubble-wrapped package was big and heavy enough to be a person. A body even. Jeez, Connie; let me please be jumping to the wrong conclusion here!

Just suppose, though, that Ecclestone had jumped Connie while she was snooping around his place. He'd panicked and done something stupidly violent, then he was left with a corpse on his hands. An unplanned murder. What would Rupert do? Call Elizabeth and confess. She would say, 'Leave it with me.' That's where the flower-delivery van and Monica would come in. They'd get the body out of Ecclestone's apartment before the cops hit the scene. Then they'd turn to Maurice Brown and his money to deal with the problem . . .

My heart was racing as I scouted along the length of the fence, looking for an unofficial way into number 165. Finally I considered a redwood pine growing inside the grounds but whose branches overhung the sidewalk. I glanced around, waited until there were no snooping passers-by, then shinned up the railings into the tree. An everyday kid getting into Huck Finn type mischief.

The thumping in my chest made me feel hot, but at the same time I was still shivering. I had to hide in the tree and wait, see what happened to Monica and the van.

Five minutes went by with the doors to the van open and the yard empty. Then Elizabeth's secretary hurried back. She slammed the doors shut, turned impatiently, went back inside.

Two minutes later she reappeared, this time with

Maurice Brown, who'd put on an outdoors, zip-up jacket, his collar turned up against the wind and hail. They both climbed into the Jacaranda van, used the turning circle and headed for the gates. They opened automatically and the two of them drove off towards town.

Thump-thump-thump; my heart knocked at my ribcage. In theory the coast was clear. Apart from the banks of security cameras and alarm systems that a guy like Brown would have in place. But I couldn't let that stop me. Inside that place, somewhere down the hotel-length corridors, in a room out of sight, there was a bubble-wrapped package that could be Connie.

9

'Kate, I'm so sorry about Carter!' Elizabeth came across with the sympathy. 'But when you think about it, it's probably for the best.'

I played along. 'Yeah,' I sighed. 'Who'd have guessed the kid had a criminal mentality? I mean, he looks so . . . innocent!'

'Do you think so?' She sounded surprised. 'Personally, I had him down straightaway as a boy you couldn't trust. Kind of rough at the edges. Not your type at all, Kate.'

'I guess I should've stepped in sooner to put a stop to the friendship.' Dad played his part. And this was difficult for him, considering he was still having trouble getting used to the fact that the woman he was recently infatuated by was probably also a major art thief. 'I knew Joey was from the wrong side of the tracks and that Kate needed to go upmarket.'

Wow, this was so unlike my dad! The guy doesn't have a grain of snobbery garbage in him. But he was cleverly feeding Elizabeth's own class prejudices.

'Exactly!' she cooed. 'And of course, Carter showed himself in his true colours when he came to my office and had the chance to put his grubby fingers on to those sketches.'

I had to grit my teeth here, follow the script. 'Yeah, well, I'm happy he's off the scene. And anyhow, there's a friend of Angel's I'm kinda interested in. He's the son of some mega-rich guy who just made a killing in the dot com world. He sells vacations on the net. The son is cool.'

'Angel Christian?' Elizabeth picked up the name right away. She dropped the caring-sharing stuff and grew bright-eyed and bushy-tailed. 'Now Sean, Angel is someone I would really like to meet!'

'Sure.' Dad's smile was strained as Elizabeth slipped an arm round his waist. 'Why not? I'll fix you an intro. Maybe you could sell her some paintings or antiques.'

'Darling!' Elizabeth gave a fake laugh. 'I wasn't thinking of it in that way. I simply imagine that Angel must be a fascinating person to talk to!'

I stared at my dad looking so uncomfortable with that serpent-arm snaked round him, and I wished I'd never logged on to that Kismet website in the first place. I mean, I wished I'd never ever got into this matchmaking stuff. A reverse wish. Couldn't someone just come along and wave a magic wand? Cancel the romance, get back to normal.

I mean, poor Dad. Poor Carter. Yeah, and poor Connie. We needed to work out what had happened to her real fast.

'So, let's invite Angel out to dinner,' Dad suggested. 'How about tomorrow night?'

Elizabeth's smiling face fell into a pout. 'Oh, darling, I can't tomorrow. Didn't I tell you, I have to fly to Europe?'

This was obviously news to him. He faked disappointment.

'But it's only for a couple of days.' She reassured him with a small nuzzle against his cheek which nearly made me puke. 'I'm going to Prague; boring business – don't ask!'

The nuzzle was about to grow intimate, so I seized my chance and made an exit from the lounge into the hall where Elizabeth had left her belongings. The plan all along was for Dad to divert her while I sneaked a peek at her stuff, looking for a clue that might lead us to Connie.

'Don't leave me alone with her for too long!' Dad

had pleaded with me. 'I may not be able to keep up the lovey–dovey stuff!'

So, after what she'd said about the Europe trip, I wasn't too surprised to dip into her purse and find a wallet containing air tickets. I was a little more intrigued to find two sets, though; one made out to Sara Hyde Smith, and one to Rupert Ecclestone, the vanishing art expert.

And I was fascinated to transfer my attention to a small travel-bag Elizabeth was carrying with her and find inside it, amongst the change of clothes, a plastic bag containing a dark wig and a pair of glasses.

'What on earth . . . !'

I was so deeply interested in the contents of Elizabeth's bags that I hadn't heard the lounge door open or seen her appear in the hall. Her voice made me drop the glasses, which hit the tiled floor and skidded under a table.

'Elizabeth, wait!' Dad appeared behind her and tried to restrain her.

She saw the wig hanging limp in my hands, the open zip on her purse. 'You little . . . !' Advancing fast, she grabbed my wrists. 'What do you think you're doing?'

It was no use covering up or carrying on the pretence any longer. I'd been caught redhanded. 'How come you're flying to Prague on a dead woman's passport?' I flung the wig at her. 'Do you really think you can get away with this?'

Elizabeth's face had assumed an intense stare and she tightened her grip on my wrists. Her eyes burned into mine. 'What exactly am I trying to get away with?'

'You tell me!' I yelled. I noticed Dad come slowly but firmly towards us. 'You and your friend Rupert have a lot of explaining to do!'

Hearing Dad approach, she let go of me and whirled to confront him. 'Your daughter's completely mad!' she insisted, trying to forestall whatever I might be about to say next. 'You should take her along to see a psychiatrist.'

'Rupert Ecclestone is more than a business associate.' He took over from me, came in with the accusations. 'You had me fooled for a while, Elizabeth, but there's a high-level, organised criminal gang at work here, and you're part of it!'

Her voice rose, she clenched her fists, but she didn't give way. 'What nonsense!'

'What's with the wig?' Dad insisted. 'What's the connection between Ecclestone and Connie Oseles' disappearance?'

Elizabeth raised her head like a startled deer. Then she went dead still.

No, forget the deer reference; it was more like a prey animal – wolf or hyena – scenting danger from a larger enemy. Time to make a rapid exit, in spite of her snapping jaws.

I stepped across the door to stop her leaving, while Dad pressed her over Connie.

That was when Elizabeth reached for her purse and took out a gun. She pointed it straight at Dad's forehead.

He froze. I had a stupid reaction; like, no way would she blow out my dad's brains. So I took a step forward. Without turning, she braced her arm and kept her aim steady. 'Make one more move and I shoot Sean through the head,' she said.

By this time I'd got the message. She meant what she said. From the totally focused look in his eyes, I saw that Dad knew it too.

'What a pity you didn't leave me any choice.' Elizabeth sighed without shifting her aim. 'I could've grown fond of you, Sean, if it hadn't been for your interfering offspring and her idiot boyfriend.'

'Put the gun away,' Dad said slowly.

She laughed. 'You mean, I should let you go? Sorry,

but no way darling. It seems my cover has been blown. Isn't that what they say?'

'I mean it, Elizabeth. Think about it. Even if you pull the trigger on me, in that split second Kate has the chance to get clean away. They'll charge you with Murder One!'

'Cut it out.' She lowered her voice to dead flat and urgent. 'Kate, come and stand beside your father where I can see you. That's good. Now, the way I see it, things work out rather differently. First I shoot you, Sean darling. Then I turn the gun on Kate. I can pull a trigger quicker than you seem to think.'

I felt Dad flinch and fall silent. We both knew that Elizabeth was capable of doing what she threatened.

'Of course, a nosy neighbour will hear the shots and call the police. They'll find two corpses in the hall and plenty of blood. But no witnesses. And by that time I'll be heading through passport control and on to the next plane out of here.'

'Elizabeth; stop. Think what you're saying!' Dad pleaded not for himself, but for my sake. He put his arm across me in a hopeless protective gesture.

'Don't move!' she cried, jerking the gun at him. 'And don't say another word, Sean. Nothing's gonna make me soften and change my mind.'

'That's right, she already killed her best friend,' I muttered.

Elizabeth swung the snub barrel of the gun towards me. For a split second I thought fury would make her squeeze the trigger right there and then. But then an urge to mock overcame her, twisting her mouth into a humourless smile. 'All right, Miss Mensa-brain; so you worked that one out, did you? It must be a small world after all. And here was I thinking that an ocean between me and England would be enough to cover my tracks!'

'Connie and I figured that you shot Sara Hyde White and stole her passport. It turns out we were right.'

Elizabeth tilted her chin defiantly and kept the gun steady. 'Sara stole my husband. I'd call what I did getting even, wouldn't you?' Her grey eyes were cold and empty at the memory.

The woman was crazy. Or pure evil, depending on your point of view.

Either way, the future looked brief for my dad and me and our exits from this life spectacular.

'The strange thing is, once you've pulled a trigger and seen first-hand the damage it can do, it doesn't seem so shocking. I mean, I had none of that Lady Macbeth conscience stuff, wringing my hands and trying to wash away the blood. No, I felt completely calm.' Elizabeth took her time to explain, as if we cared how she saw things. 'Afterwards, I realised there was no risk I wouldn't be willing to take, just to see if I could get away with it. And so, what's a little major art theft here and there?'

'Just peanuts,' Dad muttered.

'Don't be sarcastic, Sean. It doesn't suit you.' She frowned and took a couple of steps back towards the door, as if getting ready to make a quick exit.

I was thinking: *What do we do? Do we throw ourselves on to the floor and roll, hope that she fires and misses? Do we just stand here and get ourselves blasted?* My heart battered at my chest and my throat tightened. There was a click, which I imagined was the first squeeze of the trigger.

I closed my eyes and prayed.

There was a shot, a bullet ricocheting harmlessly off the wall.

I opened my eyes in time to see the front door swing open at the turn of the key. My mom had pushed it hard enough to knock Elizabeth off balance, and right that very moment she was wrestling her to the floor to wrench the gun out of her hand.

10

Whatever the urgent business was that took Monica and Maurice Brown away in the florist's van, it had made them careless.

Which was lucky for me. I mean, normally there would have been no way I could have got inside that house. But they'd left in a hurry and the service door was still ajar. As I crept into the yard I realised that they hadn't even remembered to drop the latch and pull the door shut. All that wasted heat churning out into the raw January day.

So I took the usual furtive looks over my shoulder – no one around – and slipped inside.

I was in an entrance vestibule. There was a row of empty metal dog-bowls lined up against one wall, some outdoor jackets on hooks, together with a couple of heavy dog-chains and collars.

So Maurice Brown had dogs; bad news. And from the size of the leather collars, these dogs were big. Worth avoiding, at the very least.

What's more, I was totally convinced that there must

be staff. At least one live-in housekeeper, a driver, a gardener or two. In fact, setting off from the utility area felt a lot like starting out on a new computer game; like any time, round any corner, I was about to be zapped.

I opened a connecting door and stepped into a corridor. I crouched down and began to stalk its length, expecting to meet the first enemy, looking to right and left at a row of closed doors.

Silence. I passed a room with an open door. It was Maurice Brown's gym, complete with rowing-machines, bicycles, weights and monitors. A couple of items hummed and bleeped. I jumped like an idiot and rushed on.

You're probably thinking that Mr Mogul didn't seem like a man who spent a lot of time perfecting his pecs. Me too. The guy could do with a dietician and a whole army of personal trainers to bully him into shape.

The door directly opposite led to the indoor pool. I'm not kidding. Olympic-size, fully-heated, with a sauna and cold shower section to one side. The roof was a glass atrium to let in maximum light without exposure to the elements. And there were palm trees growing in tubs and stuff.

So where was everyone? I stalked on down the corridor, round a corner, and walked into something tall, shiny and solid.

The statue didn't even wobble when I smacked into it, but it sure scared the heck out of me. It was a lifesize bronze of some Ancient Greek, and he had a six-pack to die for. His eyes were blank, he carried a discus in one hand and his metal body was bare except for some stupid fig-leaf thing.

Staring blindly across a marble hall towards the main entrance of the house, he gave new meaning to the word 'bronzed'.

Picking myself up off the cold floor, I shrugged and carried on. There was a terracotta head in an alcove, paintings of Italy on the walls. Venice; canals with gondolas, ancient arched bridges.

Surely now I would run into Security. Muscular guys would emerge through one of these doors and block my path. I'd be zapped from several directions with no hope of escape. Or the guard dogs would be unleashed. Even now they were loping down another corridor, jaws slavering, pink tongues lolling through savage incisors.

Then I realised something. Jeez, Carter, what took you so long? This was the twenty-first century, and state-of-the-art security came not in the shape of humans or animals, but as machines. Cameras. Closed circuit TV. There were half a dozen trained on me right this second, picking me up digitally and transferring my image to a control centre somewhere.

And this would be connected direct to the nearest police headquarters. Alerts would be sounded. Intruder at 165 East Park Avenue; send out an armed patrol, shoot first, ask questions later!

So forget creeping stealthily and speed things up, Joey! *Think*. How long were Brown and Monica in the house after they'd carried the bubble-wrapped package inside? Four, maybe five minutes. That wasn't long to stash the object and get back out into the yard. Which meant they probably hadn't carried it this far. I turned around and retraced my steps. Maybe the gym or the swimming pool were the obvious places to look.

By this time I was sprinting down the corridor. First I swung right into the gym, raced between the machines and monitors, flung open closet doors, searched under benches. Nothing.

Next I tried the pool. I burst through the doorway and skirted the poolside, leaping over a couple of reclining cane seats and dodging a giant pot plant. To my right, the chlorine-scented water in the pool rolled gently as directed by the wave-machine and slapped quietly against the aquamarine tiles.

My aim was to reach the sauna room and take a look

inside. And by now I had spotted the discreet security cameras set in the glass roof and knew for sure that my search time was limited.

I opened my mouth and yelled at the top of my voice. What did I have to lose? 'Connie, where are you?'

No reply, naturally. I mean, Brown and Monica wouldn't leave her comfortably reclining in one of the poolside seats, would they?

'Connie!' I yelled again. An answer in the form of a grunt or a strangled cry would do to guide me.

Still nothing. I knocked against a pedestal supporting a giant fern and tipped the whole thing sideways. The plant overbalanced and splashed into the water, gurgled to the bottom and rested there.

The inside of the sauna smelled like you would expect: scorching wood, pine-scented and stuffy. It was dark, but I could make out benches up to the ceiling, a hot metal stove and brazier in one corner. No bubble-wrapped object. I backed out, glanced into the shower cubicle, took a look at an alcove stacked with white towels and spare pool furniture.

Connie was there, propped up alongside the folded canvas umbrellas. I knew it was her, even though she was gift-wrapped, because I could see tufts of her peroxide blonde halo sticking out of the top. The second thing I realised was that she was still alive.

I mean, the package jerked and mumbled. It knocked over one of the giant parasols and tipped itself right into my arms.

'Jeez!' I grabbed it and tore at the wrappings. The tape holding them together gave way and I ripped off the layers to expose Connie's face. Her mouth was gagged with white sticky-tape, her eyes round with terror.

I had to take care when I removed the gag. It left a raised, red mark on her skin which was tender to the touch.

'Joey, thank God!' Her first words came out in a strangled sob. 'Oh, Jeez, I thought I was gonna die!'

Unwrapping the rest of her body and kicking the wrap to one side, I sat her down on one of the spare chairs. Her ankles and hands were tied tight with thick blue nylon cord. 'What happened? Are you OK? Connie, speak to me!'

'Ecclestone jumped me!' she gasped. 'I never even saw him until it was too late. I guess he'd been out, and when he came back to the apartment, he must have spotted me hanging around outside his door.'

'You're a crazy girl!' I told her. The knots took an age to untie, but at last I set her free. 'You can't just spy on a guy and set yourself up like that!'

Con took deep breaths between sobs. 'I know that now, don't I? But at the time I never expected him to jump on me from behind and half-strangle me. Did you ever feel someone's hands around your throat, choking the breath out of you?'

I shook my head and tried to stand her up, told her we had to get out of here. But she was too weak and dizzy to stay upright.

'I passed out,' she confessed. 'Next thing I knew, I was locked in some closet inside Ecclestone's apartment. He's making frantic phone calls to Elizabeth, asking what should he do now?'

'I guess she handed out good advice?'

'She said to shoot me and she'd help him get rid of the body before the cops descended.'

'Yeah, gun-happy Elizabeth. What did Ecclestone say?'

'He panicked, said he couldn't do it in cold blood. That's why she arranged to have me transferred here.' Connie looked in confusion around the storage area, then out towards the pool. 'Where am I, as a matter of fact?'

I told her and explained the mode of transport. 'Brown and the secretary dumped you and drove off in one heck of a hurry,' I explained. 'Maybe they went to fetch Elizabeth so she could be the one to actually pull the trigger on you. The others don't seem to have the guts for it.'

'Yeah, that's real comforting,' Connie muttered. This time she tried to stand up all by herself. 'What are we waiting for? Let's split!'

'It's OK, take your time.' I'd figured out that even if the cops did show up now, things would work out. I wasn't just some opportunist thief walking into the place, and I had Connie to prove it. They would listen to her story and move in on Elizabeth and the gang. Then again, what if Brown got back home before the cops?

'No, you're right.' I changed my mind and tried to hurry Connie out and along the side of the pool. She staggered and had to lean on me, but we were making some kind of progress.

Until Elizabeth Grant showed up with her neat little ladies' gun.

She stood at the exit to the pool area, taking snug aim with the glittering revolver.

The wave-machine lapped and slapped; the smell of chlorine filled the warm air.

'Stay right where you are!' she ordered in that voice which was hard to resist at the best of times.

Connie and I did as we were told.

We watched her advance. I noticed the bruise on Elizabeth's temple and two long, red scratch marks down the left side of her face. How come? I had time to wonder what had happened to her as she stepped to within five yards of Connie and me.

'Don't ask!' She read my thoughts and stretched her mouth into a weird smile. 'OK, if you must know, this temporary disfigurement is down to Melissa Brennan.'

I let my mouth fall open. Was fear making me hallucinate? Did Elizabeth just mention Kate's mom? Wasn't Melissa in New York?

'We had a fight,' she explained. 'She knocked me over and practically scratched my eyes out. But I had the advantage of the gun.'

'You shot her?' Connie gasped.

Elizabeth glanced coldly in her direction. 'Let's just say I'm here now and looking for Maurice. I have to finalise a few business details with him before I leave.'

'He went out,' I muttered, knowing ahead of time that this would annoy the lady with the gun. So I tried to be helpful. 'He left in the Jacaranda van with Monica. Maybe they went to pick up Ecclestone.'

She narrowed her eyes and appeared to do some rapid calculations. 'It seems I'd better leave them to sort out the mess they made and look out for number one,' she decided. 'I'll deal with this little problem with you two and then be on my way to the airport.'

I heard Connie gasp and take half a step sideways. I

held on to her just in time to stop her from falling in the water.

Elizabeth carried on smiling. She patted the purse which she wore slung over one shoulder. 'Tickets, passport, travellers' cheques! I can be out of here before they even find you.'

'Think twice. We're on camera,' I pointed out. 'They'll recognise you and put out an alert at the airport.'

'For Elizabeth Grant, not for Sara Hyde Smith.' She sounded confident that she could still get clean away. 'By the time they work it out, I'll be long gone.'

'Don't shoot us, please!' Connie had reached the begging stage. I guess she foolishly imagined that Elizabeth Grant had a soft centre that could be appealed to.

Not me. I knew that she could pull that trigger, no problem. You can tell that by the look in a person's eyes.

I proved my theory within a couple of seconds. Connie had just begged for our lives and Elizabeth's smile had turned evil. Then a door down the corridor opened and there was a snarling bark as two grey Dobermanns bounded into the pool area. Someone had set Maurice's dogs loose.

Elizabeth turned to train the gun on the one who came first. She aimed and fired.

The dog fell like a stone; just dropped. The bullet blasted it aside, made the grey, muscular body twist and collapse on its side. For a moment, as it hit the floor, its legs paddled and it struggled to rise. Then it lay still.

Crack! Elizabeth fired another shot. The second dog fell dead, leaking crimson blood on to the shining blue tiles.

Then Maurice Brown appeared in the doorway, flanked by Monica and an ashen-faced Rupert Ecclestone.

So much for Elizabeth's plan to look after number one. Too late for that now. I could tell from the expression on Rupert's face as he stared at the dead animals and then at Connie that he'd be putting in a strong claim to accompany Elizabeth on her emergency airlift out of Fortune City.

11

My mom is full of surprises, but this one deserved an award.

She'd got on a plane from New York without telling anyone, ignoring my instructions to let me sort out my dad's love life without her help.

Like she said to me after she'd wrestled with Elizabeth on the hall floor: 'You and your poor father are innocents abroad when it comes to affairs of the heart. I simply had to come along and rescue him from that awful woman. But it was a bad flight; a security hold-up at JFK and all. Then when I finally made it, I came up the steps and took a look through the hall window to check things out before I made my entrance – never knowing what little tête à tête I might be interrupting . . .'

'And you saw Elizabeth pointing a gun at our heads.' I got what had happened. 'Great thinking, Mom. You acted at exactly the right moment.'

We thanked her sincerely and expressed our surprise

that she could so easily handle a would-be murderess with a gun.

'Melissa, I never knew you could fight,' Dad said admiringly.

She'd actually shoved open the door and grabbed the pistol out of Elizabeth's grasp, then dropped it as she'd gone in with her fists and fingernails. Dad and I had knocked heads, scrabbling under the table for the gun, but Elizabeth had managed to hook her arms round his ankles and bring him down on top of Mom.

In the ruck that followed, Elizabeth had crawled out from underneath the heap, scooped up the weapon and scrambled on hands and knees for the door. She was on her feet and gone before we could stop her.

But no one was injured and Mom was still the hero. 'Thanks to my Japanese self-defence instructor,' she told us. 'It's down to Akiro that I learned those effective techniques.'

'Well, tell Akiro we're truly grateful,' Dad said, still rubbing his forehead where he and I had collided.

'So where is that maniac woman likely to be headed?' Mom queried. She didn't look ruffled or even smudged after her recent exertions. In fact, she looked majorly pleased with herself.

I surprised both my parents with my prompt answer.

'It's my guess, from a conversation I had with Carter earlier, that Elizabeth is making for Maurice Brown's place on East Park Avenue,' I told them. 'That seems to be the epicentre of everything that's going on.'

So we got in a cab and called the cops from Mom's cell-phone. She had a problem convincing them that she wasn't some crazy bag-lady relating her drunken fantasy to a friendly voice on the other end of the phone, until I told her to ask for Mel Wade and tell it like it was.

'Zig's brother will sort it out,' I told Dad as the cab driver whizzed us through the city centre, past Century Tower and the curved art deco facade of Fortune City Hall. 'Meanwhile, we have to work something out to get us inside Brown's house.'

Mom finished her conversation and clicked off the phone. 'Leave it to me,' she promised, before pointing out to the cab driver a route by which he could save five valuable minutes if he cut round the north side of the park. 'Take the second left off West Grand Street, down Twenty-ninth Avenue, on to East Park,' she barked.

By some miracle, we'd found ourselves a cab driver who took orders. Call it Mom's good karma if you like.

Anyhow, we arrived at the open gates of number 165

and made the guy take us up the drive and drop us at the main door. Dad was about to pay while Mom rang the bell.

'Keep your heads down until I get inside!' she hissed. 'Then when the coast is clear, find a side entrance and work your way into the house. Take a good look around while I keep Maurice talking.'

Dad threw me a puzzled look. But we did duck out of sight as the wide doors opened and Mr Brown himself appeared. The cab driver looked straight ahead as if none of this was his business so long as someone paid him in the end.

'Maurice, honey!' Mom gushed.

We could hear through the open window of the cab.

'Melissa?' Brown sounded a little unsure and definitely surprised.

'Of course it's me! Oh, I know; I should've called to say that I was in town, then we could've arranged a nice, cosy dinner *à deux!*'

'Mom *knows* him!' I hissed at Dad, my nose pressed to the cab floor.

'Kind of.' He gave a doubtful shrug, confined by the cramped space we found ourselves in. 'But not that well.'

Wow, Mom sure moved in high-up places.

'Aren't you gonna invite me in for a late drink?' she

cajoled, making out to Maurice that she was a little bit drunk. 'Just a teeny-weeny Scotch and soda and a chance to catch up on your latest acquisitions. Didn't I hear that you'd managed to get hold of a perfect gem of a Canaletto that everyone thought had been lost somewhere in Eastern Europe way back?'

Talk in the right way to Maurice Brown about the art he'd collected, and you could gain entrance, no problem.

'Fifty per cent accurate,' he boasted to Mom. 'The truth is, I've almost bought the Doges Palace Canaletto. I'm sending my people over to Prague to bring it back early next week.'

'My people'! This confirmed everything Carter and I had suspected: that Elizabeth and Ecclestone were working for Maurice Brown, who was right at the heart of this world-wide operation.

'Oh, wonderful!' Mom flattered and charmed her way over the doorstep. 'Maurice, honey, let me explain the real reason why I'm here. I wanted to see you face to face to tell you in strictest confidence that I may be able to put my hands on a sister picture to the Doges; another little known work by the same painter. How does that sound to you?'

Gobble-gulp – greedy Maurice snatched the bait. 'Come in, Melissa,' he said in a wheedling tone.

The door closed behind them and we ordered the driver to make a turn in the turning circle and discreetly drop us off in the yard at the side of the building.

Seconds later, we made it through into a utility space with coats, a boot rack, some dog-bowls by the wall.

Seconds after that, there were footsteps running towards us down a corridor leading off from the vestibule.

'In here!' I flung open a closet door and hustled Dad inside, closing the door just in time.

Two people came within a yard of where we were hiding; a woman and a man. The man spoke first.

'I'm out of here!' he gasped, out of breath from the sprint down the corridor. 'Monica, I've had it. Let go of my arm!'

Ecclestone! I took a shrewd guess, judging by the English accent and the high, strained tone. He was one jittery guy.

'I can't stand the sight of blood. It makes me heave. I've got to get out into the fresh air!'

Monica the secretary was altogether a tougher cookie. 'Rupert, get it together for Chrissakes! We're only talking dumb animals here, remember. Dogs. It's not as if Elizabeth spilled the kids' guts.'

'Not yet.' He seemed to fumble with a latch. 'But it's on the cards; you and I both know it. And no way do I want a part in the cold-blooded murder of a couple of kids!'

Inside the closet I felt my throat constrict. We had to act fast if we wanted to save Joey and Connie.

Monica obviously continued to restrain Ecclestone. 'Look, nothing's gonna happen while this Melissa woman is in the house. Figure it out; Elizabeth has to wait for Maurice to get rid of the visitor. He gives the orders, and right now he's still getting his head around the fact that she screwed up at Sean Brennan's house.'

There was a clatter of metal bowls and a scuffle. It sounded like Monica had been pushed to one side. Ecclestone was definitely on his way. 'This is one big mess,' he yelled from the yard. 'Count me out, OK. Finish, *finito*. I'm gone!'

Prophetic last words. There was a brief pause. We heard a small click, then a shot. Silence.

I was gagging and choking inside the closet, and Dad wasn't a whole lot better. We held each other's hands tight.

Monica's footsteps hurried off back down the corridor.

'C'mon!' I whispered as soon as everything went quiet again. I was out of the closet and aiming to follow Monica.

There was a small, frantic argument over whether or not we should check to see if Ecclestone was still alive. Dad went one way, out into the freezing cold yard. I went in the opposite direction to save Connie and Carter. Like, that was definitely my priority.

It wasn't hard to pick up the sound of more voices coming from an area leading off from the corridor. There were double glass doors, a domed glass ceiling, rippling water in an aquamarine pool.

And two big, limp grey dogs lying dead in pools of their own blood. Monica was huddled in conversation with Elizabeth, their backs to me. Carter and Connie were backed up against the wall.

I bit my lip and pressed myself back against the wall of the corridor. Connie had spotted me and given a small start of surprise. Elizabeth had glanced over her shoulder towards the glass doors.

Seconds seemed like an age. I heard the squeak of rubber soled shoes across the tiled floor; Elizabeth had sent Monica and her gun to investigate. So I made the only decision I could, waiting with my back flat against the wall until the secretary appeared in the doorway, her hand raised, her forefinger cocked around the trigger of the gun.

Then I did what they do in the movies: I brought

both hands down, karate-style, chopping her wrist to make her drop the gun.

Which she did.

I dived and picked it up, whirled around and aimed it across the width of the pool at Elizabeth Grant.

The big question was: would I pull the trigger?

'Don't even think about it!' I yelled at Monica, who had made a move to jump me from behind. 'You do, and I shoot Elizabeth!'

So we had me aiming at Dad's ex-girlfriend and her pointing her own gun at Carter from point-blank range.

No time to think. I squeezed the trigger and fired a shot. It echoed around the domed roof with a crack loud enough to shatter glass.

Split seconds made the life or death difference. As I fired and missed my target, Carter leaped forward with a football-style tackle and grabbed Elizabeth round the waist. She reacted by firing as she fell backwards. Another bullet ricocheted harmlessly around the pool.

I saw Connie join Carter and wrestle Elizabeth's gun from her. Leaving Monica to run off down the corridor in a major panic, I rushed in to help Joey and Connie. Three against one.

Still she made a fight. I've never seen anything like it. She was clutching her gun, sprawled on the tiles, kicking Carter off of her. She was biting and scratching at Connie like a tiger. And then up on her feet, Joey's hands round her wrist, the gun pointing towards the ceiling.

'Hold it!' I came close and tried to aim steadily with Monica's gun. The metal felt frozen into my palm; my fingers were stiff and clumsy.

Carter wrested Elizabeth's gun from her grasp and flung it deep into the pool.

I faced her. It was her against me and my gun.

Would I fire? Would I really and truly kill her in cold blood?

Her grey eyes mocked me as she took a step forward. *No way!* she seemed to sneer. *You don't have what it takes!*

She was right. My clenched hand shook, then dropped to my side. She could've walked clean away.

Except that Joey had other ideas. He came at Elizabeth again with contact-sport ferocity, this time from the side. She was thrown off-balance, flung out her arms, staggered to the edge of the water. He tried again.

It was like watching a logger fell a pine tree. Slowly but inevitably, Elizabeth tipped into the water. She broke the surface with a huge splash of foam and shooting spray and sank to the bottom. Before she rose again, Carter had dived in after her. He was there to hook his elbow round her throat when she resurfaced in a mass of bubbles and thrashing limbs.

'I can't swim!' Elizabeth gasped, choking and struggling to stay afloat.

Carter could've left her to drown, but he didn't.

He held her head above water and yelled orders at Connie and me to run and sort out Maurice Brown.

I was staring down at the gun in my shaking hand.

Connie was totally traumatized and fixed to the spot.

So Carter was the only one functioning.

Oh, and Mom, naturally. She'd acted the perfect decoy for Brown in the depths of his modern mansion until the point when the shots rang out and Monica ran to interrupt the fine-art trafficking.

Now Mom outsprinted the out-of-condition art-lover and easily beat him to the indoor pool, arriving in time to see Joey embracing Elizabeth in a synchronized swim.

'Kate, Connie, take cover!' she yelled. 'The cops have surrounded the house. I just heard a hundred sirens up East Park Avenue, so keep your heads down unless you want to get shot!'

LETTERS ON THE INTERNET

To: Kbrennan@aol.com
From: Melart@aol.com

Dear Kate,
I'm in Florence with a girlfriend; business and pleasure mixed.
How's your dad after his ordeal with the Kismet woman? Is his
heart mended yet? Poor guy; next time he wants a date, tell
him to call me. I can fix him up with someone special.
And how's the case against Maurice Brown shaping up? I
guess he bought himself the top defence attorney. But now
that the press and media have got hold of the story, even
Maurice'll have a hard time talking his way out of this one!
So, now I have to rush off to the Uffizi and ogle a Leonardo.
Take care. Love, Mom.

To: Melart@aol.com
From: Kbrennan@aol.com

Dear Mom,

Is Florence warm this time of year? We still have ice and snow here! Dad's heart is bruised but not broken. He says to tell you thanks for the offer, but next time he's looking for a date he plans to choose for himself, and face to face.

Brown is accused of art thefts totalling fifty-five million dollars! Can you believe it? Elizabeth will stand trial as his accomplice. Oh, and the British police want to charge her with First Degree Murder – of Sara Hyde Smith. She's being held in an upstate top security jail. Carter says he hopes they have a pool and teach her to swim. He nearly killed himself dragging her dead weight out of that water. They finally caught up with Monica, the sidekick driving south-west on the Interstate in the Jacaranda van. Rupert Ecclestone died before they got him to hospital, so she's up for Murder One. Neat, huh? And mostly down to you.

Love, Kate.

To: Kbrennan@aol.com
From: Melart@aol.com

Dear Kate,
I bought a Canaletto!
And no, it wasn't down to me that Maurice Brown's gang got
stitched up. You, Connie and Carter had a lot to do with it,
remember.
By the way, I changed my mind about Joey Carter. He's a good
kid. And he's nuts about you – anyone with half a brain can
see that.
Tonight I have a ticket for the opera. I need to take a shower
and get dressed.
Love to you and your dad, Mom.

To: Melart@aol.com
From: Kbrennan@aol.com

Dear Mom,
Love to Dad? Are you feeling OK? You two hate the sight of
each other, remember!
And Carter's nuts about me, huh? Dream on.
All Joey cares about is the ball game.
Love, Kate.

I e-mailed Mom every day she was in Italy. We're getting along great. I plan to spend the summer with her in Manhattan.

When I mentioned this to Carter, he didn't say much. But next time I saw him, he was paying Connie a lot of compliments and Connie was lapping it up. I suspect she wants her and Joey to be an item. Like I care!

Carter and I work well on a daily brain-level; we think similar thoughts, figure things out together. Which is how come Elizabeth, Monica and Maurice ended up where they deserved.

But emotionally I don't think we'll ever get it together. I'm watching him now, tossing a basketball to Ziggy – *run-run-bounce-pivot-throw*. So totally into it he doesn't know I exist.